DEFY

DEFY

SARA DE WAARD

DCB

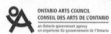

We acknowledge financial support for our publishing activities: the
Government of Canada, through the Canada Book Fund and The Canada Council
for the Arts; the Government of Ontario, through the Ontario Arts Council,
Ontario Creates, and the Ontario Book Publishing Tax Credit.

Library and Archives Canada Cataloguing in Publication

Title: Defy / Sara de Waard.
Names: De Waard, Sara, author.
Identifiers: Canadiana (print) 20240361199 | Canadiana (ebook) 20240361202 |
ISBN 9781770867581 (softcover) | ISBN 9781770867598 (EPUB)
Subjects: LCGFT: Dystopian fiction. | LCGFT: Novels.
Classification: LCC PS8607.E2364 D44 2024 | DDC jC813/.6—dc23

United States Library of Congress Control Number: 2024934029

Cover and interior text design: Marijke Friesen
Manufactured by Houghton Boston in Saskatoon,
Saskatchewan in August, 2024.

Printed using paper from a responsible and sustainable resource,
including a mix of virgin fibres and recycled materials.

Printed and bound in Canada.

DCB Young Readers
An imprint of Cormorant Books Inc.
260 Ishpadinaa (Spadina) Avenue, Suite 502, Tkaronto (Toronto), ON M5T 2E4, Canada

Suite 110, 7068 Portal Way, Ferndale, WA 98248, USA

www.dcbyoungreaders.com
www.cormorantbooks.com

to Isaac & Ava
For making the transition from when you looked up to me to
when I looked up to you lovely.

PROLOGUE

The system was not broken, but one man thought of a way to fix it. He was a powerful man — Telova Job — who was always invited to town meetings to share his insights. All government members respected him for his impressive financial success as a hardworking citizen. There was mutual benefit in this relationship as long as it remained in the public eye ... but once it hid behind closed doors, the downfall of the town became inevitable.

Before it was Zalmon, the town offered all its citizens fair, unlimited access to health care, as needed. The townspeople compensated for the enormous price tag with due diligence to use the service responsibly, volunteer contributions to the hospitals and rehab centers, and pay general taxes on purchases (back when traditional money existed).

Telova had lived an impoverished childhood with his immigrant parents, who worked countless jobs to make ends meet.

When he came of age and entered the workforce, he searched for something that could sustain him as he planned to ask for the hand of the woman he loved. The job was insurance. But it wasn't enough for him to deal with policies for life, vehicles, and property. He craved more. He yearned for that life of ease and luxury.

Telova weaseled his way into the minds of government officials, enticing them with surefire ways to earn votes. He proposed to lower taxes and ease individual contributions to society, letting private insurance companies, like his, run the health care show.

Telova was director of it all, and before long, the consortium became so powerful and money hungry that the health needs of the people were sacrificed to protect the financial bottom line. It became about the mighty dollar rather than human life.

The government crumbled and succumbed to Telova, who, in turn, established Zalmon — a place that had new ways of running things for the good of its people. It promised that under its watch, the only illness to ever plague its citizens would be Datura — a strange, uncontrollable phenomenon that can't be cured or treated. Symptoms include severe apathy, a robotic persona, glazed eyes, minimal communication skills, and the embarrassing inability to contribute to society effectively.

Things couldn't have been better for Telova and his wife, and one day, they welcomed their precious son.

INGRAIN

Excerpt from *The Book of Zalmon*:

Peter Grindin was the first Leaver. He abandoned his family in early Zalmon days — for reasons unknown to anyone who knew him, he just up and Left. Grindin's pregnant wife and two young sons were sentenced to hang in Town Square to deter further citizens from following in Peter's footsteps.

Minutes after the Grindin Three were hanged, the eldest boy's rope broke, sparing his life. His explicit, terrifying recount of his brief encounter with a Natural Death traumatizes Zalmon people to this day.

He said, "Natural Death stole my last breath, but it did not stop there. It dug its scissor-sharp nails into my flesh and ripped me open from my shoulder down my arm, all the way to my middle fingertip, exposing my veins and draining my blood. As I suffocated, chest concave, my eyes burned and summoned salt from my insides to pour down as tears into my wounds. Piercing pain sent me into electric shock. My throat choked me from within, halting hope and drowning will. The butterflies that once fluttered in my belly regressed to crawling, scratching, gnawing vermin."

Zalmon no longer executes the families of its Leavers; rather, they face the power of the shame inflicted on their legacy and the gross embarrassment to the remaining family members.

AWAKE

It's dark. Blind mice clamber along the baseboards, desperate to find cheese — or anything — to survive.

Darius Anah is too big for his bed. His buzz-cut head meets his hole-punched wall. He opens his ocean-blue eyes. His strong, seventeen-year-old limbs poke free from his bedding. He's so tired, but how can he sleep?

Darius whips off his sheets, springs out of bed, throws a pair of loose joggers over his boxers, and grabs an old white tee from a crumpled pile. He wrestles himself into it and stomps out of his bedroom.

Now in the same territory as the jittery mice, Darius tramples past them with heavy feet, and they retreat into the walls.

Walking along the upstairs hallway, Darius couldn't care less if he wakes up his mother, Sela. In fact, he throws open her bedroom door.

Sela sleeps soundly in her twin-sized bed. Her dark hair lies like tangled vines over her cheeks, sweat-soaked in place, sprawling on her snow-white skin.

Darius shakes his head in response to Sela's deep slumber. He wants her to stir, and he smashes his fist against the door frame.

"I'm out!" Darius shouts. "Not that you care."

Unbeknownst to Darius, Sela opens her eyes. She listens as her oldest child tantrums his way down the hall away from her room.

The only time Darius softens, nearly to a tiptoe, is when he is passing the bedroom of his little sister, Mahlah. She is shielded by her mostly closed door and its makeshift Do Not Enter sign, the naiveté of which tickles Darius. He stops and finger-traces the letters on the sign; he considers walking in but instead takes a sharp breath and closes Mahlah's door.

He bolts down the staircase, not without an angry flash of his middle finger directed at the mounted photo of his Leaver father.

Once in the kitchen, Darius flings cupboards open, nearly knocking them off their hinges. He takes a few canned waters and stuffs dried vegetable bits into his shirt pocket. Some sprinkle to the floor. Darius knows it's forbidden to wastefully leave them there, but he exits the kitchen anyway, much to the delight of the haggard mice.

Past the living room, just steps from his escape out the front door, Darius stops dead. He has met his match in the knowing gaze of his little sister, who beat him to it. Twelve years old and usually perfectly sweet, Mahlah stares, sour and sore, at her sibling idol. Her dark, bobbed hair reflects the moonlight that divides the living room in two.

Darius wants to retreat. Of all the people in his messed-up world, Mahlah is one he couldn't say a proper goodbye to, no matter how hard he tries. Darius eyes Mahlah's crossed arms and round fists — clenched ghost-white.

"Trying this again, are you?" she pries.

"Go back to bed, Mahlah," Darius whispers. "I just need air." He lies for both of their sakes.

"But the curfew —"

"I said, 'Go back to bed,'" Darius demands.

Mahlah is frozen in contempt. Darius uses the first two fingers on his right hand to tap her on the shoulder a couple of times. This acceptable Zalmon gesture of affection warms her, despite her best effort to stay really, really mad at him.

Darius dips past Mahlah and dashes outside.

DARE

The Zalmon clock strikes twelve. Otherwise, the city is silent with the collective obedience of its people, all tucked in bed in accordance with the nine o'clock curfew.

Except Darius, who pounds the pavement.

Muted gray windowless buildings tower alongside the plastic trees that line the streets. In the distance, Darius can see the forest of Zalmon's only real trees — sacred and off-limits — protecting the city.

Darius knows that soon the only thing between him and that forest will be the City Border. Its ever-present overhead lights reflect off the distant real leaves as they taunt him in the breeze. He looks up at the plastic trees and leaves within his grasp, their unnatural weight rendering them motionless.

It's going to rain.

Darius knows better than to be out of his house this late at night. He always knows better and never pretends not to. And he doesn't flinch in the face of confrontation; rather, he instigates it.

Darius jumps on the spot a few times, bringing his knees high to his chest. He's a rifle, pumping bullets of adrenaline and at the ready. This time it's for real. He's going to go beyond that border. He's going to rip past those real trees. He's going to Leave.

He is on his mark. He gets set. He goes.

His feet hammer the pavement. Stride after stride, Darius gains speed. He passes rows of picket-fenced houses that all look the same, especially blurred at his pace.

A half-mile into his run, Darius stops. He downs a canned water. He knows how tricky the next part of his trek will be. He needs to zigzag though the Drivers' parking lot, which bursts at its seams with hundreds of identical automobiles. At this hour, since Zalmon's residents require no rides, the cars are out of service but not unoccupied. Darius knows that the Drivers sleep for the night in their back seat cots. He has to be careful: all he needs right now is for one of those morons to wake up and play curfew-busting hero.

Darius breathes easier, because none do.

Unbeknownst to him, in one of the cars, Car 10, Driver Noah Nedab slouches in the front seat. His wide-open eyes fixate on the Zalmon newspaper headline: *Quiet End Completes $50 Million Expansion.*

The quick rhythm of Darius's gait catches Noah's attention. He tucks back into his dashboard's shadow. He scratches his bristly, full beard and watches Darius zoom by. *This kid's got heart*, he thinks, then he shakes his head.

Darius hurls himself over the last few cars, for kicks.

Past the Drivers' lot, Darius must tread carefully to dodge the far-reaching spotlights of Zalmon's pride and joy: Quiet End.

Quiet End surpasses every other Zalmon building both in enormity and architectural feat. The white marble entrances and thick, cubed-glass windows sparkle as Darius blurs past. He refuses to glance inside. There's nothing of any interest to him there. It's also no secret to anyone why people go there.

To die.

Darius shivers at the thought of their spoon-fed smiles and drug-induced calm. He can't stand their … happiness.

Beads of sweat puddle, impairing Darius's vision as he tears through one last barren fallow. The border is just ahead.

This close, the border actually disappoints Darius. He anticipated costly concrete columns, cameras, and cannons. He imagined sirens screaming at him as he approached. He prepared for a barrage of uniformed, muscular men.

Instead, he finds a middle-aged, gray-haired, fragile woman guarding a sole, pathetic booth. Maybe that's all that's needed since people are so damn afraid of what lies outside Zalmon.

Darius shuffles within ten feet of the booth. A small, red laser beam scans him. Darius doesn't react. These luminous licks have been par for the course since his birth. They pop up here and there — grocery stores, school entranceways, the Relationship Center, places like that — so of course they're here at the border. After it scans him, a widescreen device is triggered and shows tailor-made content:

First, it broadcasts a serious, put-together, dark-haired girl about Darius's age. She is tall and thin, and her name is Zuriel Levi. Her picture-perfect smile glistens. The words *Life Match* appear below the picture. Darius pays it very, very little attention.

Next, the screen shows an image of Sela, Darius's mother. The shot pans her face across the screen slowly. Darius choke-laughs and continues his walk toward the booth.

As the screen scrambles, the next ad surprises Darius. He blushes. Amid the image of some friends is an unapologetically adorable blond-haired girl named Priya. Like Zuriel, she is Darius's age. Her soft, china-doll skin glows, juxtaposed with her knowing eyes. Her head is cocked back in laughter. Darius stops and stares at the ad much longer than he should.

Standing before the cluster of real trees, Darius is the closest he's ever been to the Town Beyond. But at this moment, his mind is completely consumed by these pixels.

A downpour of rain releases from the thick clouds above. Darius lifts his shirt up over his head for protection, exposing his muscular stomach to the droplets.

The border guard exits her booth to approach Darius. She smiles.

"Out for a run?" she asks, playing dumb.

Her damn smile unnerves Darius.

She continues, "Your watch must be broken, dear." She reaches for Darius's watch, and he rips it away, jerking her wrist out of joint.

"My watch works just fine," he insists.

"Let me summon you a Driver, dear. You're a long way from home." She turns for her booth.

"I don't need a Driver," Darius huffs.

The guard holds both her smile and a stare.

Darius stares back. "I don't have to listen to you," he snorts. He gets no reaction. "Nothing can stop me from busting through those gates," he declares.

The guard tilts her head. She blinks once and holds that smile.

Darius steps right up into her face. "In fact, I could pummel you to the ground and break your neck … dear."

Just then, the screen's last advertisement cuts in like a slice to Darius's jugular. It's real-time footage of Mahlah, at home, crying in the dark on their front porch, looking anxiously from side to side for her big brother.

Darius looks at the booth. He looks at the real trees.

It's never been so possible.

He looks at the screen again. Mahlah would have a Leaver for a brother. A Leaver with no balls, who didn't even say goodbye.

Frustration erupts from deep within Darius. He screams in the face of the guard, who persists with that stare. After what feels like a lifetime, Darius retreats and turns for home. His shoulders slump in defeat.

The guard returns to her booth and lifts her one-way emergency phone as she keeps an eye on Darius off in the distance.

"Sir?" She waits, then continues. "Sir, I sent out a signal. No one came." Her hand shakes as she listens for the voice on the other end.

"There was no need to come." A deep, male voice sounds through the phone.

"Sir, the boy said he'd pummel me. Break my neck. Never in my life have I —"

"I heard everything. He's harmless." The man's voice is silky smooth.

The woman shakes her head but agrees. "Yes, sir."

Reacting to the click on the receiving end, she hangs up her device. She pulls lint from the shoulder of her uniform, straightens up, and resumes guard.

There's not a soul in sight.

CONGRATULATE

Daylight floods the Anah family's living room. It reflects off the corner of a large, white banner that hangs above a door frame. Its red, painted words — *Felix's 59th* — are bookended by hand-drawn heart-shaped balloons. Mahlah surveys her artistic handiwork as her grandfather, Felix, approves.

"I'm an old, old man, Mahlah — there it is in print." Felix laughs.

"Best old man I know." Mahlah is sincere. She double-taps him, and delight travels straight to his heart.

Birthdays are a big deal in Zalmon. There are parties and presents and, most important, the Cards. People can't wait to open the Cards. The Cards deliver Revelations from the government of Zalmon. Young people can expect such Revelations as their Life Match or the Vocation Position they'll take on from working age to retirement. People of all ages can expect to be told of any number of Life Events up to and including their pre-determined Death Date.

Today it's Felix's big day. Felix is Darius's grandfather on his father's side. Darius's mother, Sela — Felix's only daughter-in-law — walks robotically through the small crowd of guests gathered at her house. She carries trays of vegetable spreads and healthy dips. Sela is not one to mingle. She would have before she became Datura, but now she is distant and unemotional. She picks up empty glasses, heads into the kitchen, rinses them, and places them into the sink. One slips, and a shard of glass splinters from it and embeds itself in the side of Sela's palm. Sela leans on the counter, closes her eyes, exhales, and yanks it out.

"Be careful," a deep, smooth voice warns from the opposite corner of the kitchen. Out of character, Sela jumps — she thought she was alone.

Abram Job smirks. He steps out from the shadow of the pantry door. His salt-and-pepper hair is perfectly styled, and his clothes are top-of-the-line: tailored, crisp, and off-white.

Abram looks around the room to make sure they're the only two in the kitchen. He motions to Sela. "Come here," he says.

Sela shakes her head.

Abram gestures a second time; Sela relents. Abram lifts his empty glass. "May I have another?" he asks.

It's water, Sela thinks to herself. *Get it yourself*, she wants to say, but she doesn't dare. Rather, she maintains composure and fills his glass to the brim. Abram reaches out and grazes his thumb along her jawline. She steps back.

"You're so beautiful," Abram declares as he moves back into Sela's personal space. He rubs her back slowly then slides his fingertips along her spine.

Sela wriggles away. "You shouldn't be touching me this way. You know the rules, Abram," she says.

Abram bursts out laughing. Sela grabs another tray of vegetables and walks back into the living room.

Darius hates birthdays. He sits in a corner, arms crossed, and glares at the party guests in their festive party clothes with their goofy party smiles and their mundane party conversations. Then he looks at Grandpa Felix and marvels at what great shape he's still in — his button-down shirt is smooth over his impressive biceps, and his straight, white teeth shine through his heartfelt smile.

Felix sits next to Mahlah. She cozies as close to him as possible without breaking any affection laws: in Zalmon, touch beyond the two-tap is proscribed. Hugs are permitted at the Final Visit. Otherwise, bodily contact is reserved for when a married couple is granted reproduction attempts.

Mahlah loves how her grandfather smells. Unbeknownst to her, the smell is the same as her father's was. Subconsciously, it seeps into her senses and wraps her up in the time she felt her most loved … her most safe … back when her father was around and her mother wasn't Datura.

"Gramps, I have a doctor's appointment coming up," Mahlah shares.

"Annual Check?" Felix asks.

"Yeah, just a little bit early."

Felix does the math. "Everything okay?"

Mahlah leans into him and whispers, "I can't stop peeing." She giggles.

"Join the club, kid." Felix taps her twice and laughs.

Back in the corner, Darius isn't alone anymore. The dark-haired girl from the personalized ads at the border, Zuriel, stands in front of him. She flings her long, sleek hair over her shoulder, winks over at Mahlah and Felix, then insists Darius get up off his chair. Reluctantly, he follows Zuriel over to his sister and grandfather.

All eyes in the room focus on Zuriel. She looks commanding; she's a bit taller than Darius and posture-perfect. She nods hello to the other party guests, who could never match her confidence. This is her first time at a get-together at her Life Match Darius's house, yet she's remarkably comfortable.

Felix whispers to Mahlah, "Is that Zuriel?" Mahlah nods as the two of them stand up to welcome her.

Darius does what's required. "Gramps, this is Zuriel. Zuriel, Gramps."

Zuriel smiles and curtsies slightly to Felix. "So nice to meet you. My wishes."

"Thank you." Felix is charmed.

Darius is bored, so he teases his little sister. "Your birthday's soon. I wonder which boys will be on your shortlist?"

Mahlah blushes but holds her own. She deflects the question and turns to Felix. "Is now an appropriate time to ask you a few things?" she wonders.

"Good as any, I suppose," Felix says.

"What was his favorite Allowed Pastime? Reading, indoor exercising, or painting?" Mahlah loves to ask questions about their father. She was too young to take note of such things when he was still around.

"Definitely reading. Your dad never seemed to have the stamina for exercise, and he wasn't all too creative." This pleases Mahlah. She glances up at the banner she painted. She can relate.

Felix adds, pointing to Mahlah then Darius, "He sure loved spending time with you two."

Mahlah beams.

Zuriel nods emphatically, as if she knows.

Darius's eyes nearly roll out of his head.

"Why waste your time on wondering about Dad, Mahlah?" Darius says. "He didn't waste any of his on us."

"She's curious," Felix cuts in. "Leave her be."

"Well, here's the 411, Mahlah," Darius says. "He was born. He dutifully married Mom. He had two kids. He pissed off."

Felix gets his back up. "Careful, Darius. That's my son you're talking about."

"You must be very proud," Darius challenges.

"Look, I never pegged him for a Leaver either, but —"

"A Leaver for a father and a" — perfect timing, as Sela drifts by — "a Datura for a mother." Darius knows she's listening. "Lucky us."

A delivery arrives from Once a Year Treats. A party guest heads to the door and signs for it.

Inside a small confection box is one delectable chocolate cupcake drizzled with melted fudge atop buttercream icing. The lone, precious delicacy has a tall candle in the middle of it, waiting to be lit for Felix's special occasion. The guests part, and Abram steps forward to light the wick.

Darius eyes his boss and harbors hate for the fact that he's working his way into the family by spending so much time with his mother. *Why?* Darius wonders. It doesn't make sense. Darius knows that Second Matches can be solicited, but it's too weird that this relatively good-looking, able-bodied man with a steady vocation, who's never had a Life Match, wants his mother.

Darius has spent the past year in a cubicle next to Abram. He's watched this weasel-like guy stroke keyboard keys and toss intermittent papers into the Done bin. He's uninspiring, seems semi-intelligent, and is absolutely nothing like Darius's real …

Never mind.

It is what it is. This is the guy who has to put up with his mother, and Darius just has to suck it up and get used to it.

As Abram finally lights the candle, the small crowd, except for Sela and Darius, follows Abram's lead and gathers tightly around Felix to sing.

Fifty-nine years ago today,
A man came into Zalmon.
He listens and works,
And lives and loves,
And now we praise his name!
Felix! Felix! Felix!

The crowd cheers.

Darius holds his hands over his ears.

Sela is quick to clear some plates but not before Abram catches sight of what might be … a tear … in her eye? He loathes the look of it.

All Darius can do to occupy himself is stare at the Zalmon Birthday Card that sits atop a small table in front of Felix and wonder what its message reads. Mahlah grabs the Card; she's beside herself with genuine excitement to open it.

"Attention, everyone!" Mahlah yells, lacking subtlety. "Gramps said I can open his Birthday Card this year!" She sticks her tongue out at Darius, who just shakes his head. She's too cute.

A hush falls over the crowd as Mahlah tears open the envelope. She slides out a golden, embossed card with embellished edges. First Mahlah reads it to herself, then again a second time. She looks up at her grandfather and smiles.

Mahlah stands on a chair, clears her throat, and reads the Card aloud: "Dear Felix Anah. It is your fifty-ninth birthday, and we are pleased to forecast a Life Event."

Sela holds her breath. Her back is to Abram, whose smile reaches ear to ear.

Darius cringes.

The crowd leans in.

Felix stands up. "Well, here it is, folks." He clasps his hands together.

Mahlah nods and takes that as her cue to read on. "You'll soon be in the eternal company of your dear Life Match Rhonda, whom we're sure you miss so much." A collective gasp escapes the crowd. They hold their applause to let Mahlah finish. "This has been your final year in Zalmon. Your Death Date is January first!"

The crowd —

Cheers.

Felix blows out his candle.

Mahlah jumps off her chair to double-tap Felix. Party guests extend congratulations.

Mahlah silences everyone with her index finger. She reads one more thing. "Felix Anah, we at the Zalmon City Center hope you find comfort at Quiet End, where a spot has been reserved in your honor for blessed retreat."

The crowd erupts, loud enough to silence the shattered plate dropped from Sela's grasp.

Darius's jaw clenches. His knuckles drain white.

No one cheers as loudly as Abram, who holds out his empty glass to Sela to get his fill.

EMBRACE

There's a small curb in front of the Anah house. Sela sits on it with her head in her hands. Zuriel sits next to Sela and reads *The Book of Zalmon*; dog-eared pages flutter in the wind. Mahlah is on the other side of Zuriel, peeking over her shoulder every now and again to skim the words of the Book.

Darius prefers to stand.

Mahlah looks up at her brother and pats a spot for him to sit next to Zuriel as she giggles. Darius rolls his eyes but suppresses a smile.

"Are you sure you called for a Driver?" Darius breaks the silence with a question aimed like a dart at the back of his mother's head.

As if answering for her, a Zalmon car pulls up. The corner of the number 10 sticker peels off the driver's door a bit. Above it, a print advertisement boasts, Zalmon Drives — Only the Best for You.

The driver is Noah Nedab. "Off to Quiet End?"

Sela doesn't respond.

Embarrassed by Sela's trance, Darius cuts in. "Yes, we are."

Noah recognizes this kid from somewhere.

Sela gets in the passenger seat. Mahlah gets in the back behind her.

Darius waits for Zuriel to get in, but Zuriel waits for Darius to open the door for her. She tilts her head and smiles. Darius motions for her to open it herself.

The door opens from the inside as Noah reaches his hand back. Zuriel shakes her head and gets in.

Darius locks eyes with Noah, who finally places him. He's that running kid from a while back. Noah nods his head ever so slightly at Darius. It makes Darius uncomfortable, so he breaks eye contact and squeezes into the back seat with the girls.

Sela, Darius, Zuriel, and Mahlah wait in the Quiet End lobby.

Darius wonders why Zuriel couldn't pick her own damn spot. There's plenty of furniture in this expansive space, but she chose to sit on the same soft sofa as him. She twirls her long, brown hair with her manicured fingertips, engrossed in the Book as she nods along at some verse.

The lobby is picture-perfectly designed. All edges are rounded. All materials are various shades and textures of white. Framed, calligraphic, inspirational quotes dance along the walls. Expensive, smooth floor tiles glisten under Darius's impatient foot taps, which Zuriel hushes with her index finger.

The admin receptionist waltzes in, high on the fumes of a good mood, and gushes at the sight of the four of them. "Anah family?" she guesses.

Mahlah sits up proudly.

The receptionist runs her finger down a long list of names and double-checks her watch. "Wonderful! Just in time for your Final Visit with Felix."

The receptionist does a double take at Zuriel; a look of recognition washes over her. She waves, and Zuriel waves back.

"Hi, Kathy," Zuriel says. "I'm off today."

Kathy giggles. "I see that. You're in tomorrow, though." She flips to another page on her clipboard. "Four o'clock."

"Looking forward to it, as always," Zuriel admits.

Darius cuts into the mundane small talk. "So … when can we see him?"

Kathy turns to Darius and smiles. "Well, right now, dear. I'll just go make sure he's decent." She laughs as she departs.

Darius gets up and paces. His restlessness triggers the motion-activated advertisement screen on the side wall. Images of Quiet End's immaculately landscaped turf-lawn fade into and out of each other. They zoom to the grand front lobby, followed by longer shots of Quiet End's impressive, spacious suites. Next, a clip plays of joyous middle-aged Quiet End clients. They sit with their feet up, reading in a pristine, abundant library. Then the ad swipes to energized middle-aged Quiet End clients doing synchronized light exercise in a state-of-the-art exercise room. Other Quiet End clients also star in the ad, painting masterpieces on massive canvases in a studio fit for da Vinci. A narrator track accompanies the montage. *Enjoy your Final Days. Come to Zalmon's Quiet End. Find comfort in good company. Escape.*

The ad boasts smiling, pleasant workers interacting with clients in the health-food-filled, overstocked cafeteria. The narrator continues. *Quiet End's patient and attentive Personal Support Caregivers meet the needs of our valued clients.* Soft music seeps in to enhance slow-motion clips of the white-clad PSCs holding the hands of clients and leading them to a door labeled Welcome Release. The narrator practically whispers, *At Quiet End, live in peace, awaiting the Release Date personally tailored for you.*

A shot of a middle-aged client fades in. She rests, beaming, in a lush, richly upholstered armchair. She swipes her bangs from her doe eyes. *Escape a Natural Death with us. Together, we'll make your flight from this life Welcome.* The narrator's velvet voice is soothing as the woman on the screen slowly closes her unforgettable eyes and takes long … deep … calm breaths until … The ad fades to black.

Zuriel sighs. "Welcome Releases really are so beautiful."

Wide-eyed, Mahlah wants to know more. "You've seen one?"

"Sure," Zuriel boasts. "I've been promoted. I assist them almost every day."

Mahlah thinks about that for a minute.

"Well, here he is, folks!" the receptionist barks, re-entering the lobby with Grandpa Felix. Felix lets go and rushes toward Mahlah, whose arms stretch out as far as they can go. She loves her grandfather so much, and this is her only opportunity to legally soak him up in a hug.

Darius is next. The gesture of affection is awkward. He and Felix bump arms and knock noses trying to hug. Felix laughs then goes all in. Darius lets his grandfather hold him close way too long … and coughs when Felix lets go.

Felix double-taps Zuriel. She double-taps him back.

Then Felix turns to hug Sela but thinks better of it upon seeing her blank expression and cold stance. Sela looks off in the distance, fixated on nothing in particular. Felix purses his lips and, for a brief moment, revels in memories of the old Sela, happy in the company of his son. Flashes of the two of them raising toddlers and making the most out of life whiz through his mind.

"Let's head to your room, shall we?" Kathy leads everyone to a set of double-locked doors. Darius watches as she fumbles for her swipe card, finds it in her back pants pocket, and punches in her security code. She drops her card before she can open the door for all of them. As she bends to pick it up, something distracts Darius. He looks over and sees a blond-haired girl whip into Quiet End, disrupting its cushioned silence with her running shoes.

"I'm so sorry I'm late!" Priya Tiras blurts.

Darius blushes.

Kathy shushes Priya, who shuts up promptly. Her eyes apologize again. Priya catches Darius looking at her. His cheeks burn, and he looks away as Zuriel clears her throat and stands closer to him.

Darius resorts to a windowpane to catch Priya's reflection, watching from the corner of his eye as Priya dips her hand into her candy striper uniform to pull a swipe card from her bra strap.

Priya slips between all of them, swipes her card, dances her fingertips along the security buttons, and eases through the door.

"Sorry to butt in," she excuses herself, "but I'm super late!"

Priya rips at full speed down a long, white hallway, trying to tiptoe-run and failing miserably. Quiet End clients notice.

Kathy shakes her head and stops the door from closing with her foot. She smiles and holds it open for the Anahs. "After you," she insists.

Behind everyone's backs, Mahlah giggles and points at Darius's red cheeks. He swats her hand down, but not without a wink.

As Felix leads Sela, Mahlah, Darius, and Zuriel along the hallways, he waves at other clients, who nod their heads and smile. The family tours past the closed doors of the library, the gym, and the painting room.

At last, they arrive at Felix's room. It is a private room, like all Quiet End accommodations, but the suite is surprisingly tiny and windowless. It's jammed with memorabilia reflective of the many years that Felix shared with his vibrant wife, Rhonda. Zalmon got that Life Match right: the two of them were inseparable right up until Rhonda's Release a few short years ago.

Zuriel is up close and a bit too personal with a photo. "Is this your dad, Darius?" She points at a smaller copy of the same picture that hangs on the wall at the Anah house. In it, Darius's father leans on a bright lamppost in faded blue jeans, hands in the air, smiling an infectious grin with gentle eyes. A young Sela is also in the picture. She is bent over in laughter, seemingly at some wisecrack from the mouth of her Life Match.

Felix answers for the unenthused Darius. "Yes, Zuriel. That's my son."

"So, this is your room, huh, Gramps?" Darius says to change the subject.

"Yep. What do you think?" Felix asks rhetorically.

"Compared to the commercials?" Darius starts. "I think it's shit."

At that, Priya walks into the room. Darius chokes on his spit. "It's my space, and I like it," Felix rebuts. "Why, with wonderful caregivers like Priya here, how can you not?"

Priya curtsies and smiles. "Sorry to interrupt, Mr. Anah. I'll just be in and out."

Under her breath, Zuriel complains, "You're supposed to wait until the family leaves, Priya."

As Felix reminisces for his small audience, he points at pictures to illustrate his tales. He has the attention of everyone except Darius, who can't take his eyes off Priya as she turns down Felix's bed for the night.

Priya stretches her strong, defined legs. She bends to grab hold of the bed's extra pillows and walks them to a bench against the side wall. Then she reaches way over to a corner of the twin-sized bed and pulls the comforter back, all to Darius's young adult delight.

Priya turns and faces Darius. She walks up to him and timidly steps into his space to reach just past him to dim the lights. Her arm brushes Darius's cheek, and he shivers. Priya blushes. The two stand much closer than they should.

"Final Visit hours are over," Zuriel blurts. "Isn't that right, Priya?"

Priya and Darius snap to attention. Priya makes like she was busy.

"Yes, Zuriel, that's right," Priya says. "I must have lost track of time. I'm so sorry, Mr. Anah, but your Final Visit hours are over."

Zuriel beams. "This is a wonderful moment."

Darius watches as Priya mimes another apology then excuses herself.

Zuriel walks over to Darius and taps him twice. Reluctantly, he taps her back. Then Zuriel smiles at Felix. Her eyes are filled with admiration, knowledge, and what seems like a hint of jealousy. "My wishes." She curtsies then steps into the hallway.

Darius turns to his grandfather, suddenly hyper-aware that this is the last time he'll ever see him. A foreign pain plagues his tight chest. He doesn't know what to say. He panics and instinctively looks to his mother for guidance. For a moment, he actually thinks he sees an expression on her face. A frown, maybe? Darius blinks his eyes hard then watches as his mother just turns and walks out of the room. He rubs his temples. *For crying out loud, Mom, nothing?!*

Felix senses his grandson's agony. He doesn't want Mahlah to be influenced by it, so he scoops her up in his strong arms one last time and spins her around and around.

"Wow!" Mahlah laughs from deep in her belly. The laugh echoes through the Quiet End hallways and into the resting hearts of all the clients. She throws her arms around her grandfather's neck and squeezes so hard that Felix has to catch his breath.

Felix steadies Mahlah back on her feet. "You're a born leader, darling. You're destined for great things, you know."

"I know." Mahlah nods.

"Get going now, love." He taps her twice, out of sheer habit. Mahlah dismisses the taps and hurls herself forward for one more of those hugs. Then she does as she was told and walks away.

"My wishes, Gramps!" Mahlah calls over her shoulder before she joins her mother and Zuriel in the hallway.

Now it's just the two of them.

Darius doesn't look up. Felix doesn't make him.

"Our last couple of Outside Visits have been really great, kid," Felix reminds Darius. Or maybe he's reminding himself. "They just don't like us to drag this final one on, you know?"

"Why can't we see you again?" Darius asks.

Felix shrugs. "Just the way it is."

"But you're still scheduled to be here for a while. We could come see you and —"

Felix rubs the top of Darius's head, taking liberties. "It's okay."

"Maybe we could apply to have you live with us until your Release," Darius presses.

Felix laughs. "I'd just get in the way."

"But ... are you happy here?"

"Sure." Felix rocks back on his heels.

"You can't be serious," Darius blurts.

From out in the hallway — and out of character — Sela says, "That's enough, Darius."

"Oh! It speaks!" Darius says.

"I'm only here a handful of weeks," Felix reminds him, "so what does it matter?"

"Yeah, right. I mean, we're only talking about dying here!" Darius has to look away.

"Darius, I choose peace and to avert a Natural Death."

"Yeah, I've read the Book, thanks." Darius wipes his eyes and holds his hands over them.

Felix wraps his arms around Darius, holding him much like a bear would, mauling him into submission. Darius tries to break out. Felix holds him tighter. Darius twists and turns then tears free.

A wild pain rips through his heart, and he leaves.

DIAGNOSE

The doctor's office waiting room is sprinkled with patients of all ages contentedly watching their personalized birthday ads loop for them on a screen. Smiles plaster their lips, giving Darius, who sits next to Mahlah, reason to snicker in the corner.

Annual Checks for Zalmon people are compulsory. A Driver is dispatched to the person's house about a week prior to their birthday to take them to and from their doctor's office. Under absolutely no circumstances can a citizen miss or reschedule their appointment. Everyone in Zalmon knows it and can't pretend otherwise.

However, Annual Checks can happen sooner than normal in some circumstances. Such is the case today, with Mahlah's. She's simply adhering to Zalmon's protocol, as is outlined clearly in the Book: *If you experience any physical or mental symptoms contrary to preteen normality, you must consult your doctor as soon as possible.*

Darius didn't like the idea of Mahlah going to their doctor's office alone, so he took the day off work to accompany her. This waiting area is as far as they'll let him go, however, and when a nurse calls for Mahlah to enter through the side doors, Darius is left alone to scrutinize his environment.

The receptionist behind the glassed-in counter is Datura — obvious from her apathetic stare and robotic actions. Darius wonders when she caught the plague. His mother came down with it roughly five years ago; she wasn't born that way. No one is born with it, and as far as they know, it's not hereditary, although some family members do seem to catch it at the same time.

The receptionist turns her head slowly to look at Darius, who chews his fingernails and spits a piece of one in her direction. Of course, she doesn't react.

Someone enters the waiting room, and the receptionist drops a pile of papers. Darius looks up and is surprised to see Abram, his boss — and also the man who doubles as his mother's Second Match. But Darius barely recognizes Abram with his graying hair so windblown and his suit so uncharacteristically disheveled.

Darius looks away. No one wants to talk casually to their boss — even if he's only slightly superior — on a day off, let alone lock eyes with their mother's current lover. He shudders.

Abram spots Darius yet doesn't seem surprised to see him. "Hello, Darius," Abram says as he slicks his hair back in place.

There's no avoiding him now. Darius nods acknowledgment.

Abram helps himself to a seat next to Darius and takes aim at his personal life. "How was the Final Visit last week?" he asks.

"Ask my mother." Darius smirks.

"I'm asking you."

"It was bullshit." Darius snorts. The receptionist coughs.

Abram laughs. "Tell me how you really feel, son." The term of endearment shocks Darius.

"I'll never be caught dead in that place," is all Darius can think of to say.

Abram laughs again. "Take one of your Abaters, Darius. You're all out of whack." He stands and buttons his suit jacket. "I will see you at work tomorrow."

"What brings you here, anyway?" Darius asks. "It's not like you to miss work, and your birthday's not until May."

Abram smiles. "How nice of you to remember." Then, rather than answer Darius's question, he says, "You think too much, son."

Darius cringes. Abram doesn't leave the building. Instead, he enters the door to the examination room hallway without a nurse's solicitation.

"Hey." Darius snaps his fingers at the receptionist. "Why does he get to just go in there?"

The deer-in-the-headlights Datura doesn't respond.

In one of the rooms, Mahlah sits on a bed looking at one blood-tested, cotton-balled, bandaged arm while a blood pressure gauge is strapped around the other. Her legs hang over the edge of the plastic mattress and drum a beat against the thin, wobbly aluminum frame. She fiddles with her backless blue gown and gives it an extra tuck under her bottom.

The doctor walks in. He's mid-thirties, lanky, and prematurely bald. "I'm sorry I left you in here for so long. A colleague needed a second opinion."

"No problem." Mahlah shrugs.

The doctor puts his glasses on to read and record Mahlah's blood pressure results in her folder then re-coils the arm strap before dropping it in a holster. Next, he puts his stethoscope earpieces in place and holds the metallic end to assess Mahlah's lungs through her back. She knows the drill and takes plenty of deep breaths. He puts a checkmark on the page.

"So, what else, Mahlah?" he asks.

"Well, I'm so thirsty. Like, all the time," she admits.

"I see." The doctor scribbles a note then flips to a chart in the folder. "And you're almost thirteen."

"Yep!" Mahlah bursts.

"Have you been taking your Inhibitors since your First Blood incident?" he asks.

The question makes Mahlah blush. She doesn't know why, but for some reason, she feels awkward talking about anything to do with when she bled down there. It was the strangest thing the first time it happened, even though she'd heard about it every year in school since first grade. Her teachers would address the girls in the class, right in front of the boys, and tell them that there would come a day when they might find some blood on the toilet paper when they wiped themselves, or maybe they'd find some in their underclothes. They didn't tell them why, or when it would happen, just two things: that it would happen without a doubt and that as soon as it happened, you must tell your mother and make an appointment with your doctor immediately.

"Yes, I've been taking my Inhibitors," Mahlah assures him.

"And no more incidents?" the doctor asks.

"None."

"Great. That means they're working."

The doctor skims his notes. He lifts his head from the page and takes a good look at Mahlah. She smiles at him. He smiles back then clicks a rubber stamp dial a few notches and stamps her folder. He reaches over into a wicker basket and hands Mahlah a Golden Delicious apple. She devours it.

The doctor is alone in the examination room, starting to clean up for the day. He separates a stack of folders according to their stamps. The great majority of them are piled to the left while just two are tossed to the right.

Mahlah's is the last folder for the doctor to sort. He tosses it onto the big heap on the left just as the door opens.

The doctor looks up and pales at the sight of Abram. "Sir?" the doctor squeaks.

Abram puts his index finger to his lips to hush the doctor then closes the door. "As you were, doctor." The doctor relaxes only slightly as Abram reaches over and grabs Mahlah's folder.

"Sir, I have never seen you … I mean, it's not often that you … check in like this."

"Mahlah Anah is a special interest case." Abram sifts through her paperwork.

The doctor speaks up. "She's Category Two, in my opinion." He stands. "Manageable, sir."

Abram zeroes in on a few lines of text. "Over 140 milligrams per deciliter? Frequent urination? Fatigue?" He eyes the doctor. "Do you have her blood work results?"

The doctor turns to the last page in Mahlah's folder and points.

Abram reads it and then goes over to a laminated paper on the counter. He runs his finger down a long column of numerical data and stops near the bottom.

"$1,310 per annum? We can't have any of that." Abram laughs. "Not Category Two; definitely Three. Understand?"

Abram's words snuff the spark from the doctor's eyes. He barely manages a, "Yes, sir."

"And write it in this year's Card," Abram orders as he chucks Mahlah's folder into the smaller pile on the right.

"But, sir, she's only —"

"Age is insignificant, regardless of norms. Not to mention that your 'but, sir' borders on insubordination, doctor." This shuts the doctor up, but Abram continues. "Very few citizens have such privileged access to classified information. You are in a powerful decision-making position with protocols and prompts. To question things on account of some kind of ... I don't even know what to call it — subjectivity — is ludicrous. Need I make an example out of you?"

The doctor averts his eyes like a shamed puppy post carpet accident and sits back down. He shakes his head, then remembers to add, "No, sir."

Not convinced, Abram stomps over to a very high, steel-barred cupboard and jabs a ten-digit security code into the keypad protecting it. It opens. He reaches in and pulls out a tiny metallic computer chip.

Abram holds the chip up to the doctor's face. "I suggest you exhibit more respect toward that honor and that trust, doctor."

The doctor doesn't say a word; a bead of sweat trickles down his forehead as he fixates on the small microchip. He bows ever so slightly and nods in compliance.

Suddenly, there is a commotion in the hallway.

Abram and the doctor open the office door in time to see a blue-uniformed orderly dragging a bloodied, sheet-covered corpse down the hallway. The expression on the orderly's face is as blank as the front-counter Datura who follows him, mopping up a trail of smeared blood.

Abram inquires with a mere lift of one eyebrow.

The orderly responds, "No witnesses, sir," as he turns down a long, twisted hallway then through a door marked Incinerator.

Abram sighs. "It must be a full moon." He motions to Mahlah's folder. "Keep up the good work, doctor," he demands, then leaves.

The doctor takes Mahlah's folder in his hands. He slips off his glasses and rubs his baggy, watery eyes. He grabs a pen to scratch out the existing stamped message then reaches over for the rubber stamp, clicks it slowly a few notches, and re-inks the folder. He places it onto the smaller pile then stands at his computer.

The doctor's fingers shake as he selects Mahlah's profile on the screen and begins to type.

STUDY

This Way High School is quaint. The hallways boast the paintings of its students. The lines in the artwork are mostly straight. The colors all primary. The strokes methodical. There are no twists of a Picasso, no pulse of a Basquiat. No one's about to cut their ear off any time soon.

Zalmon teachers are borderline Datura, or at least that's the running joke. You might think there's a slight shimmer in their eyes, but one blink and all goes black.

This Way High School is the only high school in Zalmon, and strict memorization with subsequent regurgitation renders critical thought useless.

The classrooms contain rows of desks with right-angle indicators etched onto the floor tiles indicating the exact uniform placement of the legs. Each desktop has a built-in screen, optional keyboard, unidirectional microphone for dictated responses, and a wrist guard for ergonomics.

A student's typical school day consists of four hour-long subjects: Chronicles, Individualized Vocation Training, Homeostasis, and Relationship Management. Students have two half-hour breaks and one hour-long lunch.

Chronicles outlines the history of Zalmon as recounted through the Book and some approved supplementary texts. The Book contains the observations and revelations of the initial Wanderers who found and settled Zalmon. Every citizen of Zalmon is gifted a copy of the Book in Year Two of learning. They are not expected to carry the massive, thousand-page hardcover publication with them everywhere they go, but if they're ever caught without the condensed pocket summary in their possession, they are forced to make a public apology then retreat to the publishing house to retype the entire contents. Only a handful of Zalmon citizens have ever been known to commit the infraction.

Individualized Vocation Training teaches students their future job responsibilities and how best to contribute their skills to society.

Homeostasis deals with the notion that each citizen shall eat, move, and live with the goal of a stable equilibrium between all interdependent physiological elements. In other words, they learn that they are what they eat and that their bodies are temples that require a healthy balance to obtain physical actualization on all levels.

Finally, every student's favorite: Relationship Management. The students sit in close quarters with their peers and the instructor, keen to learn of the permitted goings-on in granted relationships. Depending on their age, they learn about everything from First Blood and Inhibitors to the preparations for permitted procreation seasons with their Life Match, and eventually the forever dreamed-about Peak Spasm, which, according to teen talk, is going to blow their minds. The older students also receive lessons on mutual respect, acceptance, suppression, and surrender.

It is lunch hour now. A group of seventeen-year-old boys, including Darius, sit with their Life Matches on some wooden stools off to the side of the cafeteria. Most of the girls work on their Chronicles assignment about Peter Grindin.

The boys taunt the girls for studying when it's social time.

"Grindin was the first Leaver, blah, blah, blah. Put your notebooks away," one boy says.

"He up and left his pregnant wife and two young sons. We all know someone like that, don't we, Anah?" Another boy taunts Darius and laughs.

Darius ignores him, but his friend isn't having it. "How'd you like to hang dead from your neck like Grindin did?"

A collective "Oooooooooooh" erupts from the onlookers.

"Could you keep it down?" Zuriel says as she looks up but holds her place in the Book.

"Oh please, Levi, you've got it all long memorized," a boy says. Darius laughs.

"Of course I do," Zuriel says. She points at the group of girls. "But they need all the help they can get." The girls shoot a look of sympathy in Darius's direction. He doesn't notice — he's carving his name into the side of his wooden stool with a fork. He's half-listening to a side conversation going on between another two boys.

"It's badass down there," one of them says.

"Why?" the other probes.

"Because they don't give a" — he looks around — "shit. There's loads of junk, synthetic enhancers, forbidden contact. Everything."

"Are you talking, like, real forbidden contact?"

"Yeah, screw the taps! Skin on skin. Holding it in their hands. Putting it inside!"

The boys readjust themselves.

"It's got to be an urban legend."

"No! It's somewhere. I know it."

"The Book would tell us to beware of it if it were real."

"How would they know?" The boy laughs.

"Spies."

He laughs harder. "Spies? Espionage and our slogan: Zalmon Trusts?"

Darius leans in. "You asses talking about the Underground?"

The boys' eyes widen. "You know about the Underground, Darius?"

"It's bullshit," Darius huffs. "Sorry to bust your tent poles, boys, but trust me, I've been looking for it since I was twelve. Does not exist."

Darius gets up. He's had enough of this banter. He needs to stretch his legs. Zuriel notices nothing; she's too enthralled in the Book.

Darius walks along the hallways as kids his junior sit unenthused in their classes, picking their noses and staring off into the black dots of the sound-absorbing ceiling tiles.

He turns down the Facilities wing of the school. He likes this part. No one is ever around. The maintenance and cleaning staff do their thing at night.

Darius hears a kind of rhythmic, scratching hum coming from the room next to the mechanical room: the lounge area for the night staff. He recognizes the sound but can't place it. His curiosity draws him there.

When he gets to the open door, he peeks in and is surprised to see Priya in the dark room on a stationary bike. Her light hair is tied up into a messy bun atop her head that wiggles from side to side as she pedals vigorously.

Priya senses that someone is there. Panicked, she tries to stop her feet, but the wheels keep whizzing. Afraid of being caught and punished, on account of exercise not being her chosen pastime, she turns her head slowly to check over her shoulder.

Darius steps into the dark room as the wheels yield to quiet. Priya is slightly relieved but noticeably apprehensive. Still, she approaches him.

The two of them find themselves in a familiar position — standing a couple of feet apart. Neither of them says anything for what seems like an eternity.

Priya breaks the silence. "You know, Darius, you really shouldn't look at me like that."

Darius shies away from the eye contact. "I don't know what you're talking about, Priya."

"Look at me," she whispers.

Darius does.

"Yep. Like that."

Darius feels a smirk slip out. "You sure flatter yourself. I know who my Life Match is."

"And I know mine, so … that's that." Priya wipes the bike seat down. She turns and walks away.

Then she stops and turns back around. "Your grandfather, Felix, he seems happy, by the way. He seems at peace with his upcoming Release."

Darius pretends he's not sweating it.

Priya adds, "I just think you looked uneasy is all."

"Yeah?" Darius shrugs. "Well, maybe you shouldn't look at *me* like that."

Priya blushes.

"Are we going to ignore the elephant in the room?" Darius asks.

"Who you calling an elephant?" Priya says playfully.

"Seriously, Priya. Why are you in here?"

"I like exercising," she admits.

"Then choose it as your pastime," Darius says.

"I chose reading."

Darius smirks at her honest reveal of dishonesty.

"And if you must know, I paint too," she says.

Yes, he must know. Darius leans in to hear more.

"When the Quiet End clients turn in for the night and it's my duty to clean their common areas," Priya says, "my favorite moments are when I'm alone in the painting room and no one knows I'm there. I'm invisible for what I can imagine to be a lifetime. In darkness, except for the light from the tip of my flashlight, I brush paint into summer sunsets or autumn frost footprints, winter forest hikes or spring buds bursting on the branches of the Town Beyond's trees."

Darius opens his mouth but says nothing.

"Are you going to rat on me?" she asks.

"Zalmon Trusts —"

There's something about the way that she laughs at this that launches Darius's thoughts into oblivion.

They hear oncoming footsteps and know what's best. After a long glance that neither intended, they part ways and sneak out opposite exits of the room.

OVERRIDE

Darius sits at his work cubicle, third in a row of cubicles within rows of cubicles, intersecting a column of cubicles within columns of cubicles. The particleboard separators are an even-toned gray. The plush carpet hushes footsteps. No personal accessories adorn desks. The distraction-free employment zone forbids any kind of socialization. They can't get to know one another, so one has only one's mind to take one away from the monotony of work.

Darius's workplace processes data pertaining to the consumption of electricity by the citizens of Zalmon. The government caps the flow of power to homes, even though it's harvested internally, because it needs the excess to run its government establishments. There are families that surpass their limits. To warn them of their infraction, an electricity moratorium is imposed on the residence, and everything goes to black. It doesn't last particularly long, but it's enough to deter most people from further overuse. All power abuses are noted, quantified, and compounded until fines are issued. Payback consists of supply labor in other fields, most often fulfilled by the adults of the household, like covering the vocations of child-bearing women as they tend to their newborns for the first six weeks (deemed a long enough term by the leaders). The extra hours to cover a woman's maternity leave would be worked above and beyond your normal duties.

Darius's assignment at his workplace is to ascertain what appear to be ghosts: unexplained overuses of power that can't be pinpointed to specific houses. Something is off. Every year, there's escalating consumption, but the amount of people in Zalmon never changes. Is there a leak? What accounts for the losses?

Darius stares off into space as his right hand enters data into the computer from pure muscle memory. His fingertips are little soldiers that blast each key into submission. An occasional prompt appears on the monitor, to which Darius screen-touches a response. And repeat. All evening long. Such is his Vocation Position.

Abram leans way over to Darius, who is mid-yawn, holding his jaw wide open for as long as possible. His eyes water before he lets it go, but not without a disruptive and dramatic roar of release.

"I had a Mid-Annual the other day. Sure sign I'm getting old." Abram laughs.

Darius shrugs and keeps typing.

"Just, you know — to answer your question. It's why I was there at the doctor's office," Abram lies as he walks over to Darius's cubicle.

"I forgot I asked." Darius touches the screen, flips a paper in his stack, and continues typing.

"Oops," Abram says exaggeratedly. He throws his hand atop Darius's to stop its pattering. "You missed one."

Darius locks eyes with Abram as he backspaces, enters a long string of numbers, then touches the prompt on the screen blindly.

Abram snickers. He pushes. "Your mother invited me to Mahlah's birthday celebration."

Darius hits the keys harder.

Abram taunts, "You don't mind your boss hanging around at your family events, do you?"

Darius says nothing but thinks, *Only slightly superior.*

"Come with me for a second, Darius," Abram suggests. "I'd like to show you something."

Abram leads Darius down corridors that he's been restricted from since day one at this job. All of the walls and floors and ceilings look the same to Darius, and he's curious why Abram knows it all so well. He didn't pin him for having this kind of access — the kind that's reserved for whoever's in charge.

So Darius is even more surprised when the two of them encounter a locked steel door down a long hallway and Abram taps his card and enters a code into a keypad beneath the handle. The door clicks open.

The room is the size of a gymnasium. One wall is filled with active computer screens full of code. In the center of the room is a long metal counter with empty chairs that face the screens.

Abram boasts, "Welcome to Central Processing for the Relationship Center."

Darius hates to admit it, even to himself, but he is impressed. He knew this room existed, but he had no idea it was hidden in the same building he's worked in every day after school since he was fourteen.

"Here?" Darius asks.

"That's right." Abram says.

"And you know the code?"

Abram laughs. Darius wasn't joking.

As Abram walks along the counter, he flicks it with his index finger then rubs his fingertip to see if there's any dust. There isn't.

Darius is perplexed. Did they just break into the place? If so, and if Abram admitted to it, Darius would have a lot more respect for —

"Sit," Abram orders.

Darius does, but only because he's tired of standing. He looks closer at the screens.

Each is adorned with avatars of Zalmon citizens engaging in various levels of relations. The Relationship Center exists because prolonged physical contact between people is strictly forbidden beyond times like conception duties, but Zalmon knows humans have inherent needs. For a fee, people can visit the Relationship Center for artificial experiences to prevent acting on their sexual needs out of turn.

Zalmon capitalizes on the desires of its people. Thousands of paying customers line up daily at the headquarters, spending big to be able to manipulate the movements of their avatars to experience heightened levels of sexual arousal.

The realistic sounds of relations between the AI contacts are muted, but Darius has a very hard time not peeking at the visuals. He has to turn away in fear of being physically stimulated.

How embarrassing would it be to have such a response in front of his mother's Match, of all damn people?

Darius is suddenly aware that many of his buddies are probably at the Center right at this moment, some on their one evening off, exchanging their hard-earned currency for five minutes of entertainment. Darius begins looking for avatars of individuals he recognizes, they're so lifelike, but Abram flips a switch that causes all of the screens to go to black.

"You know who I engage with when I visit the Center," Abram says.

Of course Darius knows. There are rules. You can't just go around engaging with whoever you want. But why? Why would Abram make Darius think about this?

It looks like Abram has a list of options before he uploads an avatar of Sela. Darius wants to question it, because he's never seen something like that before, but he's too busy gagging a little at the sight of his mother in a tight, revealing dress.

"Why, Abram?" Darius asks. "Why are you showing me this?"

"Even though I'm not her original Life Match, I care for your mother very much."

"Cool." But it's not cool.

"I plan to be with her for a very long time."

"Why?" Darius laughs.

"Why?" Abram questions.

"It's one thing to have" — Darius makes quotation marks in the air — "'patience with, pity for, and possession of' someone and be their Second Match late in life, but she's Datura. She's been mentally impaired since my father Left. She's just ... Why, Abram?"

"I didn't mean to upset you, Darius."

Darius resorts to a familiar shrug of his well-trained shoulders. "No sweat," he adds for effect.

"I'd never try to take the place of your father."

Darius doesn't bite. "Take it. I don't give a shit."

"Such a shame he was a Leaver. Sometimes people just don't have what it takes to deserve the good life. They can't live up to what's expected of them, even though it's more than fair. Fatherhood is not … for the weak of heart." Abram's phone vibration interrupts the lecture. He shields the caller ID from Darius. "I have to take this," Abram says as he rushes himself and Darius out of the room.

Abram holds his phone to his ear while struggling to tap his card then punch his password into Central Processing's door keypad again.

"Just a second," Abram barks into the phone as Darius bumps into him. Abram drops his phone and bends to pick it up while he motions a patronizing flick of his wrist to scoot Darius back to work.

Darius obeys as he tucks the card he just swiped from Abram's pocket into his own.

Abram storms the opposite way down the long hallway.

Darius marches in the direction of his cubicle until he's sure Abram is out of sight, at which point he turns back toward Central Processing's metal door as he mouths a sequence of numbers over and over.

Darius looks all around to ensure he's alone. He reaches into his pocket and grabs the security card. He taps it on the reader and enters Abram's security code, which he memorized. The door clicks open. Darius slips inside.

To Darius's delight, in Abram's haste, he forgot to log out of his account. Darius mocks his mother's stationary avatar before he helps himself to a chair, cracks his knuckles, and proceeds to type, slowly at first, then eagerly.

Life Match + Priya Tiras?

At the touch of a button, the command processes. An image of an unsuspecting, seemingly innocent young man appears.

Darius recognizes the avatar as a boy he knows from school. "I knew it! Loser." He laughs out loud then types feverishly, glancing back at the door every so often. He hits one last key, then the system responds with:

Cannot Change. Life Match Algorithm Resubmission?

Darius types.

Y-E-S

An intricate computer programming script blankets the screen. It's Greek to Darius. He falls back against his chair.

"Damn it." Darius escapes the program. He slumps in his chair, but then an idea sits him up straight again.

"Mahlah's thirteenth is this week!" he says to himself. "Who's my little sister's lovey-dove going to be?" Darius giggles as he types.

Mahlah Anah + Life Match Candidates?

The computer beeps and a prompt appears.

Redirection: Mahlah Anah Card

A thumbnail of his sister appears. Her smile lights up the room better than any other projected image can.

"Redirection? All right. Maybe I need to start there." Darius hits the enter key. He rechecks the door, then turns his head back to the screen, eager to read Mahlah's list of upcoming Pre-Matches — the three boys who, as a fringe benefit as her older brother, Darius gets to torment for the next couple of years before Zalmon makes one of them official. The screen does not disappoint.

Mahlah Anah Life Pre-Matches: Salin Drod, Cartier Ronin, and Drine Stile

Darius surveys the dorky thumbnails of Mahlah's potential life partners and holds his stomach in laughter. He scrolls down the page.

Vocation Position: Childcare Practice (Destination: Elmwood)

Darius smiles; they got that one right. Mahlah would be a perfect fit to work with children. He taps the arrow key a few more times to reach further down the results. But he freezes. His ocean-blue eyes widen at the words on the screen.

Information Override:
Mahlah Anah Death Date
Set December 15th

Darius gasps. Her Death Date? His mouth dries in horror. This has got to be some kind of massive error. He shakes his head in disbelief and re-reads the screen over and over.

He tries all of the commands he knows to delete or reverse the information.

Unsuccessful and now in a fit of rage, Darius hits random keys, hoping to rectify what is before him, but the screen yields the same message.

Information Override:
Mahlah Anah Death Date
Set December 15th

"There's no way!" Darius hollers.

There is commotion out in the hallway.

Darius kicks the chair out from beneath him and stands. His fingertips torment the keys in synchrony with the booming beat of his heart. He scours his brain to recall codes from years of his vocation. Finally, the computer beeps.

Delete Dath Date?

"You're damn right delete Death Date!" Darius can hardly breathe.

A herd of steps approaches the metallic barrier between Darius and dire consequence. Still, he types.

Y-E-S

As the doorknob rattles, Darius exits the program, returning the screen to Abram's lone avatar of Sela, just waiting to be manipulated. Darius slides under the counter to hide from the group of Central Processing workers who enter the room for their shift.

SILENCE

Darius sits in the corner at school. He put himself there to try to flush out the bad thoughts that continue to run rampant in his head, thoughts that rip at his heart and force a pain unlike anything he's ever felt.

My baby sister is ... dying? plays on repeat.

It wasn't easy for him to escape Central Processing yesterday. He had to wait out the workers while they did their duties on the equipment. He had to sit through their disgusting comments about the avatars once they got the system back up and running after Abram's flip of the switch. Their unprofessional banter regarding the "better" moves they'd perform on the avatars was revolting.

But through some quick thinking, patience, quietness, and the grace of a relatively dark room, Darius managed to escape.

Knowing that Mahlah's days are numbered paralyzes Darius in

all-consuming sadness. Beyond stalling the delivery of her Card, there's nothing he can do about it. He's sure that the powers that be will eventually figure out what happened, and he doesn't know how much time he has.

Those damn Cards!

The notification of her demise will no doubt ignite everyone's gleeful acceptance of the fact that they're losing the best person in Darius's life. They'll see the Card as an enlightened exit. Darius will see the Card as he saw it yesterday — agony.

But intercepting Mahlah's opportunity for a peaceful passing at Quiet End and exposing her to the horrors of the Natural Death that must be looming has left Darius struggling. He has never been so torn about what to do — leave it as he left it or admit to what he's done? His stomach flips and flops. It twists into convulsions and makes him sweat.

With his head in his hands, Darius doesn't notice Priya two feet ahead of him, stepping into his space.

Priya sits down and takes out her homework, making as much noise as she can.

Darius looks up. His usual glance of adoration has been replaced with a scorn that takes Priya aback.

"Why do you work there?" Darius blurts.

"Oh, hello, Darius," she says.

Darius is not in the mood for play, and he replies with an intense stare.

"A lifetime of service at Quiet End is my Vocation Position," Priya says, as if she's rehearsed it.

"Appeal for something else."

"I don't want to," Priya says. "Your Life Match works there. Ever tell her what to do?"

"It suits her." Darius glances around, wondering if Zuriel's lurking nearby.

"It's a good enough place, Darius," Priya says.

"Whatever." He shakes his head. "They all go … Datura in there."

"That's ridiculous," Priya snorts. "They don't go Datura. Daturas are useless; they're brutal."

"My mother's Datura."

Priya bites her tongue. "I'm so sorry. I didn't mean to —"

"Whatever," he says dismissively.

"Has she been that way forever? Or …"

"Since I was twelve," Darius says as matter-of-factly as he can muster.

The two of them go quiet. Eventually, Darius speaks: "When my time's up, I'll wait it out for a Natural Death."

"You're crazy."

"That, or I'll Leave."

"Leave?!" Priya erupts. "Nice. Leavers are assholes."

"Asshole's in my blood."

"Why?"

"My father Left."

Priya softens. Her eyes show she cares without resorting to pity. "Mine too," she says. "When I was two."

Darius had no idea they had that in common.

The quiet returns, heavy and absorbing, until Darius breaks it again.

"I woke up early one morning and snuck down the hallway. I used to like watching him get ready for work. I'd study how he lathered his face in shaving cream and mimic how he glided his razor over it. He tapped me goodbye that morning just like he had any other morning. Just as if all he was doing was going to work. He galloped out the front door without looking back. I wasn't even worth a second thought."

"See? Asshole," Priya says.

"Before that," Darius continues, "my mother was so … perfect, you know? She'd wipe Mahlah's bangs from her eyes, cut our fruit slices into smiley faces … She actually tucked me in."

Priya moves forward a bit. Darius moves back.

"It's the stupid shit you remember," he says. "After my dad Left, she caught Datura pretty much instantly. I don't sweat it, but it's been hard on Mahlah."

Mahlah.

Darius chokes up. He's had more than enough. He shoots upright and walks off, leaving Priya alone in a cloud of silence.

DISENGAGE

Sela stands still, dead center, in Abram's office. To the right of her, there is a massive birdcage imprisoning a beautiful gray bird. Sela looks at it when it makes a soft trilling noise.

"It's a mourning dove," Abram says.

"The cage wasn't enough?" Sela says as she notes its clipped wings.

Abram laughs. "It's a rarity. There used to be all kinds of them around, before the changes."

Sela makes eye contact with its soulful, beady black eyes.

Abram sits behind his massive mahogany desk with his bare feet up. He stares at Sela, who can't take her eyes off the bird. Abram leans over to dim his office lights to a soft glow, then he reaches back to turn on some instrumental music.

"I'd like you to dance for me, Sela," Abram requests, his voice smooth like caramel.

Sela glances up at him and shakes her head.

Abram's smile fades. "Dance, Sela."

Sela swipes a strand of hair from her eyes and holds her head higher.

Abram puts his feet down.

Sela dances.

She looks back down at the floor as she sways her hips ever so slightly to the left and then to the right. Her arms hang heavy at her sides as she manages to move her torso up and down with as little effort as possible.

"Look at me while you dance," Abram commands.

Sela brings her eyes up to meet his. Her stare is a fiery glare from deep within. She manages to move even slower, controlling her every movement with tightened muscles and intensity.

Abram sighs and stands. As he approaches Sela, her movements halt. She straightens.

Abram is in her personal space. He reaches up and glides his fingers along her neck.

"That's against the rules," Sela reminds him.

"I am the rules." Abram's fingers graze the nape of Sela's neck then dip into the top of her blouse.

Sela frowns and looks away.

"Look at me," Abram orders.

Sela won't. Abram widens his fingers and clamps them tightly around Sela's neck. She slips away. Abram yanks her back.

Sela goes still in Abram's hold. He moves her dark hair back from her shoulder to expose her ear. He breathes along her lobe and kisses it, then continues soft pecks onto the sensitive skin behind her ear where there's a small, skin-colored bump. He encircles the bump with the very tip of his slimy tongue.

"Still in place." Abram laughs at his inside joke.

Sela doesn't move. Abram clears his throat then purposefully talks into the small bump. "Disengage. Code alpha eight, beta fourteen, delta six."

Sela appears even more scared now than she was a moment ago. She tries to minimize a gulp as it passes down her throat.

Abram caresses Sela's face and glides his thumb over her bottom lip. "Alone at last," he whispers.

"How convenient."

Abram belly laughs. "You're sounding an awful lot like your son. If I didn't know any better — if I didn't know everything — I'd think he was the first non-Datura to know about your little" — he fingers the spot behind Sela's ear — "secret."

Abram leans forward and kisses Sela's lips. Hard. Dry. Daunting.

Sela jolts away from Abram's face and spits on his feet.

He grabs her arms and pulls her even closer than before, battering and bruising her pale, fragile arms.

"Now, Sela," he starts, "I expect you to behave like a good little Datura. You do what you're told without resisting. Understand?"

Sela's eyes water.

"For starters," Abram directs, "take off all of your clothes."

DEFLECT

The Anah house is at capacity with so many friends and family members gathered to wish sweet Mahlah the happiest of birthdays, anxious to hear what's in her Card.

Mahlah practically floats around the room, naturally high on the love and attention. She wears an eccentric outfit that she put together for the occasion, which includes items from all three of the clothes closets in the house. Her imagination is no-holds-barred in the way she wears Darius's baby-blue tee off one shoulder, Sela's ancient, thick beaded belt and old necklaces, and her own white leggings that she cut the hems off. Everything is misaligned and mismatched, but Mahlah crushes the look.

Zuriel double-taps Darius as she walks by him then sinks into a spot on the sofa. She munches on a plate of veggies.

Sela drifts in and out of the room with colorful platters of high-vitamin foods in hand, serving unemotionally and bowing to her guests. Abram stops her to pick at a tray.

Darius paces the length of the room with rapid strides, emoting signals of deterrence to any social souls who want small talk with him. He wipes his clammy palms on the sides of his faded blue jeans. He dreads the reading of Mahlah's Card, the details that he may or may not have interrupted.

The Card sits on a well-lit pedestal in the middle of the living room. Mahlah eyes the Card with a vastly different anticipation from Darius's.

Zuriel steps up and blocks Mahlah's view of her prize. She teases Mahlah with a whiff of the luxurious, sugar-filled cupcake that's just been delivered from Once a Year Treats, which rests next to the Card. Playing along, Mahlah leans forward to smell it, but Zuriel yanks the cupcake away and laughs as she stabs it with a candle and lights the wick on fire.

The crowd, all but Sela and Darius, erupts into song.

Thirteen years ago today,
a girl came into Zalmon.
She listens and works,
and lives and loves
and now we praise her name!
Mahlah! Mahlah! Mahlah!

The crowd claps, cheers, whoops, and hollers.

Zuriel hands the cupcake to Mahlah. "My wishes," she offers.

But Mahlah declines. Abram raises an eyebrow. No one passes up their chance at the sugary, delectable, unhealthy indulgence they're permitted once annually.

"No thanks, Zuriel," Mahlah says. "I'm feeling a little …
funny these days." Mahlah couldn't care less about the cupcake.
She stretches her neck to see past Zuriel and focus intently on
her Card.

"Mahlah! This is the only junk food you can have until next
year. Dig in." Zuriel holds the cupcake in Mahlah's face.

"I know." Mahlah smiles but ignores the offer. She runs to
the center of the room and picks up her birthday envelope from
Zalmon's leadership. Abram takes it upon himself to quiet the
room with clinks on the side of his glass.

Darius feels sick to his stomach. He wipes sweat from his
brow. He bolts to Mahlah and swipes the Card out of her hand.

"I'd like the honor, little sister," Darius declares, barely holding back vomit.

The crowds *awws* in unison.

Zuriel rolls her eyes.

Abram chomps on a carrot.

Darius clears his throat and swallows a lump the size of a
football. Mahlah motions for him to just get on with it already.

Darius's hands tremble as he struggles to open the envelope.
Once he does, he hesitates.

"Darius!" Mahlah laughs. "You're driving me nuts!"

Darius is lost in the math of how many more days he'll be
able to see that incredibly sweet face. Why are her days numbered? What is happening? Will this Card notify everyone of his
imminent, heart-wrenching loss?

Well aware of Mahlah's growing impatience, Darius pulls the
Card up to his eyes. He skims it.

Abram smirks.

Darius exhales. He closes his eyes to hold back tears, opens them again, and reads, "Dear Mahlah Anah. It is your thirteenth birthday, and we are pleased to forecast these Life Events."

Abram stops mid-chomp.

Darius continues. "Your Life Pre-Matches are: Salin Drod, Cartier Ronin, and Drine Stile."

Mahlah screeches and hides her red cheeks behind a sofa pillow. Some people in the crowd giggle.

Darius revels in his sister's innocence.

Abram frowns.

Darius reads on. "Your Vocation Position is Childcare Practice at Elmwood."

Mahlah shouts, "I love Elmwood!"

The room erupts in cheers. Darius holds the Card high above his head and waves it to and fro for the crowd. He flings it across the room then runs down the hallway into the washroom, slams the door closed, and vomits into the toilet.

Back in the living room, Abram rams his way through the tight crowd to search for the Card. He finds it in the corner behind a side table that he has to squeeze beside. He picks it up, reads it over, and clenches his fists as his pupils dilate, rendering his eyes pure black.

PUNISH

Abram busts into the doctor's office reception area, nearly ripping the door from its hinges. Splinters fly across the waiting room, but the Datura receptionist just minds her own business.

Inside his examination room, the doctor hums as he files a folder and tidies a few supplies.

His door flings ajar and smashes the wall behind it, puncturing a doorknob imprint into the plaster. Abram pounces and grabs the doctor by the throat before throwing him on top of the supplies.

"Zalmon runs on subordination!" Abram yells into the doctor's face. His breath fogs the doctor's glasses lenses.

"Sir?" the doctor manages with what little breath he's afforded. He shakes in Abram's hold. His arms are frozen at his sides.

Abram lets go of the doctor's throat but looms over him with barely an inch of space between them. "One year alone! One year, for that girl, is more than the expense of three Final Years for seniors."

"I … I don't know what you're talking about," the doctor says. "Pardon?"

"Sir. I don't know what you're talking about, sir," the doctor whimpers.

Abram grabs the doctor's shirt collar, whips him upright, then heaves him forward and back again, beating his head hard against wooden shelf corners.

"The forecast — for Mahlah Anah. You didn't update it after I told you to do so." Although Abram's voice is calmer now, it elicits even greater fear and discomfort in the doctor.

"I … I'm sorry, sir. So sorry. I'm sure I … I thought I —"

"You're sorry? You thought? Now we have to wait a whole year. Did you even stop to consider the costs? Let alone the risk to Zalmon if" — he lowers his voice for fear of anyone else hearing — "she passes unexpectedly? The risk of possibly having to silence another?"

The doctor shakes his head profusely. Words fail him.

Quietness lingers.

Then a shift.

"Speaking of silence," Abram laughs, "perhaps I've made the grave mistake of trusting you."

The doctor panics. "Sir, my deepest regrets, but I —"

Abram turns toward the high, barred cupboard and enters the complicated code into the keypad. "It's been ages since I've done one of these myself," he says as he reaches in for a tiny metallic piece and holds it gingerly between his finger and thumb.

The doctor tries his luck. "I'm sure there is some logical explanation, sir."

Abram won't have it. He pushes the doctor over a stool, and he lands on the patient bed. The doctor struggles to get back up, but Abram's massive forearm pins his neck to the bed and holds him in place.

Abram's pressure on the doctor's neck stifles his vocal cords. The doctor gasps for air while his face turns crimson; blood rushes to his cheeks, nose, and ears. Sweat trickles down his forehead and into his eyes. He reaches frantically for an emergency button on the wall.

"Who you hoping to summon, doctor?" Abram laughs. "Your Datura receptionist?"

Grave defeat consumes the doctor's eyes.

Abram kicks the doctor's arm away from the alarm with the steel toe of his boot. Bones shatter. The doctor can't scream, but his protruding eyes speak volumes.

Abram pinches the metallic chip between his index finger and thumb. He whispers into the doctor's ear as he slices a razor-thin sliver into the soft bit of flesh behind it. "It was just a matter of time before you let me down."

The doctor squirms like a fish on a hook. Veins bulge beneath the surface of his skin in deep shades of purple and blue.

"Seems I'm short on time, doctor. I'd have loved to call in anesthesiology." Abram laughs as he jams the chip deeply into the doctor's wound, past a layer of fat, and nestles it in a pool of tissue and blood.

The doctor passes out.

Abram lifts his forearm and checks the doctor for a pulse. He smirks and taps his cheekbones a few times.

"Why make things so difficult, doctor?" Abram asks facetiously. "You'll be all right in the morning, and of course I'll

know it. I'll know every little thing you say or do from now on."
He laughs again.

Abram reaches into a drawer for a surgical stapler. With
bloodied fingertips, he folds two pieces of the doctor's neck skin
together and then pumps a few staples in.

"I'd run through all the Datura rules for you, Doctor," Abram
says, "but you co-wrote them." He laughs once more as he walks
over to the computer and types.

Finally, Abram takes a tissue and dabs away the blood from
behind the doctor's ear. He admires his work before he leans in
closer and says, "Engage."

Abram peeks over at the computer screen briefly, then continues. "Alpha ten, beta thirty-six, delta nine."

STRAY

Darius should be at school, but he doesn't care, and no one else seems to care either.

His feet are as heavy as his heart. It's the eve of his sister's Death Date, according to what he read that fateful day, and the weight of the world rests on his shoulders. Darius hasn't told a soul about it. No one would believe that he intercepted it, not to mention that someone would most certainly turn him in.

Darius has been watching Mahlah with burning eyes, looking for signs of a looming Natural Death. Darius has never known — never even heard of — someone who has died a Natural Death, other than reading about it in the Book. Zalmon uses its incredible resources to advise people of their Death Date in advance so that they can avoid a terrifying Natural Death and instead free themselves to the next chapter via a comfortable, earlier Welcome Release at Quiet End.

Zalmon citizens deny Natural Death the chance to torment and snag them.

Darius selfishly opted to spend time with his sister rather than lose her to Quiet End for her Final Days. He spent every waking moment he could with her, soaking up every second.

Knowing it's happening tomorrow, Darius's decision to interrupt Mahlah's Card weighs heavily on him. There's no doubt about it, he denied her a peaceful departure. Darius being Darius, he wonders if he has what it takes to save her from a Natural Death. He's not sure. He's not sure about anything.

What will it be? What will take her?

It can't be a car accident. Traffic is a well-oiled machine backed by timed streetlights, padded medians, dreadfully slow speed limits, and assigned drivers with 100 percent assurance ratings. Car accidents are myths or folklore, like the Underground. Parents tell their kids about vehicle accidents like ghost stories — to get them to sit down and behave in cars rather than act like wild animals.

Speaking of which, it can't be a death from that either. There are no venomous or carnivorous animals to fear in Zalmon like the ones the Book warns about from the lands beyond the Edge.

Also, there are no murderous citizens like there were in pre-Zalmon times.

So, what else is there? What else could possibly terminate his Mahlah other than old age, which is far off in her future? Young people may Leave on rare occasions, but they never die.

Of course, Darius can't talk about this to anyone. He wonders if people would be equally as distraught about Mahlah's Death Date had he left it in her Card. Or would everyone have just gone on their merry way, singing her birthday song and finding delight in her residence at Quiet End before an early Welcome Release?

Darius's fists are tight. There's a permanent wrinkle on his forehead from furrowed brows. His blue eyes are perpetually moist from constant threatening tears.

Mid-thought, Darius stops dead, finding himself right in front of the Zalmon Relationship Center. The building is seldom busy this time of day because seniors have their discounted slots in the morning, the adults line up after work, and kids Darius's age prefer to go on weekends or much later at night. Still, a few people, mostly men — always mostly men — linger around the Center, pretending to debate whether or not they'll head in, just like Darius seems to be doing now, except he's not pretending. Is going into the Relationship Center really something he'll do in a moment of inner turmoil like this?

Darius looks around and makes eye contact with a Zalmon driver sitting stationary in his car. It's that Noah guy.

Noah nods his head slightly to acknowledge Darius, who looks away. Noah eventually starts up his car and drives away.

Moments pass before Darius unzips his backpack and pulls out his Relationship Center card.

This activates an electronic billboard close to him, showing two avatars: his and Zuriel's. The avatars embrace each other tightly until the projected image fades to that of a massive beating-heart icon.

Darius waits in an orderly, efficient line in the sanitized, all-white Relationship Center. He peers at yet another commercial monitor that plays an ad just above a man's head as he leans on one of the turnstiles. It shows a picture-perfect couple waiting in a doctor's office. The woman is dressed in a plain blue hospital gown and lies on the bed, smiling incessantly at her husband, who stands at her side before he lowers himself onto the bed beside her. A voices narrates the scene: *Conception Cards: the Zalmon blessing for Life Matches to procreate.* The ad fades to show the couple in a pristine hospital room. The woman is on the bed again, and a doctor is extracting a baby from between her spread-open legs. The ad cuts to the same man and woman now holding their toddler's hands. They fling the child high up into the air, contented by his giggles. Narration sounds again: *In Zalmon, we know how important touch is before the age of three.* The mother scoops the little boy up into her arms, kisses his face all over, and spins him around and around. *After that, we respect touch prohibition.* The husband double-taps his Life Match's arm as the words The Zalmon Relationship Center swipe in. *Visit the Zalmon Relationship Center today for all of your interpersonal needs.*

Then the ad fades to black.

Darius finds it odd for that particular ad to play for that guy here. What is the purpose? Maybe the lie-down part elicits physical excitement and desire in some visitors. Maybe the mere thought of the ultimate blessing that permits Life Matches to engage in sexual intercourse is enough to cause these line-ups and encourage spending. Darius just doesn't get it — maybe because his Life Match is Zuriel.

Darius is now near the front of the line and observes the service counter employee — a busty, dolled-up woman who smiles at the customers and leans over ever-so-suggestively for upsells. This particular Vocation Position is usually assigned to Zalmon's Lookers — the universally acknowledged beauties of the land who take to makeup most effectively. It's not a glorious occupation, especially because at a certain point in their lives, when their good looks fade, they're transferred to Relationship Center Maintenance and Cleanup.

Many men blush as they submit their plastic cards to the Lookers for verification and tracking. The girls attempt to keep things flirty and fun. Darius has noticed a stark contrast in reception, though, when the odd shawl-covered female customer approaches the counter. Those times, the counter girls sit back and punch in the information stoically, avoid conversation, and avert their eyes. Rather than hand the admission ticket to the women with a slow, gentle double-tap on their arm, as is customary with the men, the tickets are practically thrown across the counter.

"Next?" a Looker calls out to Darius.

He clears his throat and approaches her, head low.

"One-on-one room?"

Darius nods.

"I'm going to need to verify you, hon."

Darius hands her his plastic card. She looks it over then swipes it through a reader. She looks at her monitor. "I see you don't come very often," she observes.

Darius looks down at his feet. He searches for … An excuse? A reason? Something witty? Nothing.

Her monitor beeps. She points to her left and says, "Room number four. Please come again."

She hands Darius his ticket and double-taps his forearm two times with a lingering sensation. His goosebumps have a mind of their own.

Darius heads toward Room 4.

⌒

The room is dark.

The walls are velvety-soft, thick, deep red curtains that enclose the small booth-sized area, except for a massive screen that takes up one whole wall. There is a small counter between that screen and Darius. As Darius sits on the stool at the counter, a ticker brings its daily visitor count to thirty-five.

Darius squints to read a short list of directions etched into the countertop. Then he proceeds to hover his right hand over a protruding black semicircular heat sensor.

At this, the screen activates, and the words *Identified Need: Stress Relief* illuminate the room.

Darius yanks his hand from the sensor and shakes his head. He wants it to pick up on his normal teenage sexual tension. He takes a deep breath and tries again.

Identified Need: Stress Relief.

"Fine!" Darius succumbs.

Name: Darius Anah scrolls across the bottom of the screen just as an avatar with an impeccable resemblance to Darius looms and turns to look directly at its controller.

Life Match: Zuriel Levi appears at the bottom of the screen as Zuriel's strikingly accurate avatar springs up and stands next to Darius's. She walks forward and starts to massage his shoulders.

Darius frowns at the screen. He rips his hand away from the sensor again and feels around the underside of the countertop. His hands locate a small, concealed door about the size of a safety deposit box. Darius tries to open it, to no avail.

Darius turns and reaches into his backpack. He shuffles things around until he finds a fork from his paper bag lunch. He jams the end of the fork into the teeny slit of the small compartment door. Darius pulls down hard for leverage and …

Nothing. The damn thing won't budge. The avatars of Darius and Zuriel stare ahead, awaiting directions.

Darius kicks at the miniature door. He kicks it again. And again. Harder and faster. Over and over.

From outside, a disgusted Looker side-eyes the banging sounds coming from Room 4, imagining what could be happening inside.

After one final kick fueled by years of pent-up frustration and teen angst, the small door surrenders. Darius jerks it open and is pleased to find a keyboard inside. Without hesitation, his fingertips stroke a stream of keys, and in no time, the screen reads *Create New Avatar?*

Darius nods.

"Oh yeah," he says as he continues to type, even faster than before, whipping through various prompts as the avatars freeze in confusion. Darius compels Zuriel's avatar to disappear outright as his onscreen self faces an onslaught of changing females. The screen invokes things like eye color, hair color, hair length, height, weight, age … all of which Darius answers until an avatar astonishingly close to the likeness of Priya stands in front of Darius's.

Darius can't help but smile at his work.

The prompt *Name?* turns up.

Darius shivers for a second, then types, *Priya.*

He is pleasantly surprised by the computer's response.

Insert Priya Tiras from database?

Darius hesitates. He looks toward the booth door, back at the screen, then back at the door before he smashes the enter key.

Nothing happens for what seems like an eternity.

"Did I break it?" Darius mutters to himself.

He is about to give up and leave when a sequence between Darius's and Priya's avatars begins. Darius leans back in his stool a bit, tantalized by the onscreen images, which he plans to enjoy intimately.

On the screen, an open field is blanketed with lavender and calla lilies. Priya walks along in a flowing, white, partially see-through lace top and faded blue jeans. Darius sneaks up behind her and whispers something in her ear. Priya blushes and turns around.

The two are face to face, inches from each other. Darius leans in. His lips graze Priya's. She holds the sides of his face and looks deeply into his eyes. They touch lips again, this time teasing each other's tongue tips.

Darius's hands slide down Priya's back, slowly, then move all the way down to her thighs. He pulls her in close so that her body is tight against his. His fingertips trace the top of her jeans, then he lifts up his top and hers so they can press their bare bellies together. His chest is tickled by the cotton of her bra.

Darius peppers kisses all along Priya's neck and down into the valley of her chest then back up to her lips, deeper than before — passionate as she grabs his hair and they lean in hard against each other.

Darius's hands wander down again to Priya's jeans to undo the top button. Darius unzips her zipper as —

Bold, red words interrupt: *Action Restricted. Must Earn 18-year Card.*

Darius hammers down on the keyboard, but nothing changes on the frozen screen. The crimson words taunt him. Darius slams his fist hard on the sensor and shatters its glass. He rips the small compartment door off its hinges and throws it. It smashes the screen and leaves a gaping hole between the Darius and Priya avatars.

A Looker storms into Room 4. She takes one peek at the vandalized booth and calls out, "Security!"

ABATE

Darius sits across the kitchen table from Sela. His arms are folded, and he leans way back in his chair, testing its legs with all of his weight.

"Take it, Darius," Sela says as she motions toward the small white pill in front of her son. It lies next to a foggy, half-empty glass of water.

The pill is an Abater. Darius has been taking this medication since his father Left. As far as Darius can tell, there are several different kinds of tablets. He knows the most common one from his Relationship Management class: after a female's First Blood, she has to take Inhibitors to cease further blood spills. She only stops taking them when she enters the Preparation Stage of Procreation. In Chronicles class, Darius learned that before the creation of Zalmon, societies didn't care. They just let women bleed monthly, making them endure excruciating pain and public scrutiny over their hysteria and scarlet uncleanliness. The Book explains that the bleeding signified irresponsibility at the hands of the governments because any woman, post First Blood, could become pregnant. As such, the societies didn't regulate their populations to ensure equal opportunity and liberty. Darius knows Mahlah takes her Inhibitors every single morning — at the beckoning of the noisy alarm clock set to remind her.

Another tablet Darius knows about are Minimizers. Zalmon claims these pills quell a person's false sense of intellectual superiority. According to the Book, out of their control, some citizens become critical of their environment and can be overwhelmed by untrue internal thoughts. For example, the kids who speak out in class with a train of thought so far off the track, heads turn. Or people who garner a reputation for spewing wacky theories or fabricated accounts. Before these people can sway the thoughts of others, their Minimizers squash erroneous points of view. Darius knew a kid at school once who was like that — he wouldn't shut up about fictitious Underground tales, and people got tired of it. The pills have a calming, almost Datura effect, but unlike Daturas, people on Minimizers function socially.

Finally, there are the tablets that Darius is on. Abaters are emotional inhibitors meant to calm nerves and hush outbursts in members of society who can't regulate such surges on their own. Many of Darius's buddies are also on them, but strangely, he's never known a girl to use them. Maybe they're just more discreet about it. Regardless, Darius feels Abaters are senseless for him: he can control himself — he just doesn't want to.

"Darius, your pill. Now," Sela urges.

Darius shakes his head and leans further back on his chair. The legs splinter.

"You caused a lot of damage in that small room today." Sela hasn't strung this many words together in a long while.

"Isn't that my thing?" Darius huffs. "Damage?"

Sela's eyes are cradled by puffy, dark bags. She rubs hard circles over her temples.

Darius baits her. "Look, I have a lot on my mind." He hopes some kind of inquisition will follow. After a thick silence, he concludes, "But you don't care, so why would I bother talking about it?"

"Darius, take your pill —"

"It's December fifteenth tomorrow!" he yells. His eyes water.

Sela just stares at her son.

Darius jumps off his chair. "And I feel like I can't even tell you, my own mother, why that date even matters!" He bolts forward, face to face with Sela's stone-cold expression. "Ask me, damn it!" he flares. "Ask me why it matters!"

Sela moves her hand from her temple and places it over the small bump behind her ear. She speaks softly and ever so slowly. "Take the pill, Darius."

Darius slams his fists onto the table.

"If you don't," Sela practically whispers, "they'll have to find another way."

Darius pulls Sela's hands away from her head. "I'm so sick of your shit," he yells. "Your predictable, Datura bullshit!"

"They'll use something else to keep you … quiet," Sela says, and just as she says it, she flinches hard and cranks her neck. She holds her hand over the bump again.

Darius's chest puffs. He's equipped to blast her, but he is caught off guard by her trembling. He watches Sela rock herself through some kind of pain, which makes him uneasy.

He grabs the small white pill, tosses it to the back of his throat, and drowns it with water. He whips the empty glass against the wall, and it smashes into a thousand pieces.

He slips past his mother and out of the room.

SURVIVE

The sun sets slowly on the horizon. Pink, wispy clouds sprawl overhead and seem to reach out and touch the Anah backyard.

Darius rolls out a couple of sleeping bags onto the ground and arranges them side by side. He flicks off rogue blades of fake grass from them.

Mahlah watches her brother set up camp and beams.

"It's a rare treat, having you to myself all day like this," she says as she smiles at her big brother. "And we've spent so much time together this past while."

Darius would smile back, but he can't. Every second of this day, he's been consumed, awaiting the very moment a Natural Death will strike his sister. He refuses to leave Mahlah's side, knowing that Zalmon said that today is the day she'll die. His relentless conscience knocks him silly on the inside, knowing she could have averted this with a Welcome Release at Quiet End.

Darius feels bad enough that he selfishly surrendered to having his sister endure a Natural Death; there's absolutely no way he'd let her experience it alone.

"It's nothing," Darius replies. "I just thought it would be fun to camp out here all night. Like old times."

The sun has long set. The stars twinkle. Mahlah yawns.

"It's hard for me to stay up late these days," she says.

Darius doesn't want to talk about it. He has noticed his sister has been much more tired. Weak. Pale. This must be how it is when one's end looms. He's always noticed, expected, and been at ease with such conclusions for old people, but his Mahlah? The voices in his head curse the leaders of Zalmon.

"Remember how against tents Dad was?" Mahlah laughs. "'Tents, shments,' he'd say. I may have been little, but for some reason, I'll never forget that." She giggles and is compelled to double-tap Darius's arm.

He turns his head away so she doesn't see his eyes water. "I'm sorry, Mahlah."

"Sorry for what?"

So many things, he thinks, but he goes with this one: "I think he Left because of me." Darius has never admitted that out loud to anyone before. "For some reason, I can't help how I am. Who I am." Darius shakes his head.

"Whoa, heavy!" Mahlah laughs. "What's with you?"

Darius stammers, "It's just … I'm just —"

"The Book says we never know what makes people Leave." Mahlah throws him a rope, of course. "But I think we should forgive so we can move on in Zalmon's comfort."

The last thing in the world that Darius wants to talk to her about right now is the Book.

"This has been the best day ever." Mahlah sighs.

Darius gulps. "No sweat." He checks his watch. It's nearly eleven — the final hour on the day of his sweet sister's demise.

Mahlah lies down and pulls her sleeping bag tight to her chin. Her eyelids are unbelievably heavy, but she's pushing hard to stay up late with her big brother. She looks up at the stars.

"Ever wonder what it's like out there?" she asks.

Rather than look up, Darius looks to his right and focuses on Zalmon's border in the distance. "Always," he admits.

Mahlah drifts off.

Once in a deep slumber and oblivious to the rules, she snuggles right up against Darius and half-smiles in her sleep.

Darius double-taps her gently on the back. Then he throws caution to the wind and hugs her tight. "Goodbye, sweet girl," he whispers. "I'm so sorry for this coming pain I've caused you." He succumbs to a waterfall of tears.

Darius rubs Mahlah's back in full, loving circles, despite being forbidden to do so. He watches Mahlah's chest rise and fall with every single breath.

He wonders which will be her last.

The trilling sound of a bird nudges Darius awake. Before he can place what the sound is, the thing takes flight and disappears.

Darius squints as sunbeams pierce his formerly shaded eyes. For one blissful moment, he forgets where he is and why he's there.

He lifts his head from his … pillow?

Which is, in fact, Mahlah's back.

Darius's stomach turns. How could he fall asleep on her in her most dire time of need? As if he wasn't awful enough already!

Darius turns his head slowly to face his sister's closed eyes, blank expression, and motionless body. He rips away from her, runs fifteen feet away, thrusts himself into the bushes, and throws up.

"Mom!" Darius hollers between heaves.

There's no response from within the house.

Darius gurgles another gut-wrenching cry for his mother. "Mom!"

"What's wrong?"

Darius whips around.

Mahlah stands in front of him, perfectly alive.

Darius hyperventilates. He spins back around to throw up some more.

"Are you okay, Darius?" Mahlah asks.

"Are … are … are *you* okay, Mahlah?" Darius reaches for her cheek to feel if she's real. The touch surprises Mahlah. She gently pulls his hand down and looks around to make sure no one is watching. She shrugs. "I'm a bit hungry."

Darius steps backward. He stumbles on some twigs and falls.

"Darius?" Mahlah giggles.

Darius holds up a finger to silence Mahlah before he runs full-speed into the house.

LISTEN

Darius tears into his mother's bedroom.

Sela jumps out of bed.

"What are you doing in here?" she hollers uncharacteristically and grabs for her robe. "Get out!"

"Mom, I need you," Darius admits for the first time since he was small. The hairs on his arms stand at attention. His heart pounds like a jackhammer.

Sela is frightened by his urgency. "Let's talk in the kitchen."

"Who cares what room I'm in?" Darius says, clenching his teeth. "What's the matter with you? It's about Mahlah —"

Sela covers the side of her neck as best she can. She crouches down and points to the hallway for him to get out.

Darius yells, "Stand the fuck up and listen to me! Mahlah's Card … it was supposed to say —"

Sela punches the side of her neck over and over. Darius has

heard about Datura outbursts like these but has never seen one in person. He runs to his mother and grabs both of her wrists, causing her to whip her head from side to side and screech nonsensical words at the top of her lungs.

"Don't pull this Datura shit with me now! Mom — I saw something —"

With a strength that surprises both of them, Sela frees her hand from Darius's grip and clamps it over his mouth to shut him up. Darius bites her index finger, and she pulls her hand away.

"I saw something I wasn't supposed to see," says Darius.

Desperate, Sela headbutts Darius, cracking the bridge of his nose. As blood flows from his nose, he flies back into a shelf of framed photos that all come crashing down.

Sela screams and starts picking up objects and throwing them around the room.

Darius wipes the pool of blood from his face with the sleeve of his white shirt. He dodges airborne knick-knacks and old perfume bottles. He drops to the floor and crawls over to the bedroom door then out into the hallway.

Sela slams her door shut behind him. Darius turns and smashes his fists against the door repeatedly, until splintered panels bloody his hands.

Sela falls against her door and slumps to the floor. She muffles her sobs as best she can.

Darius runs through his house then flies out the back door. He zooms past Mahlah, who swings on the back rocking chair, humming an old hymn from the Book. She spots Darius, smeared in blood.

"Darius! What happened?!"

"Nothing," Darius says. He whips around the side of the house, then out front. He is about to summon a driver when he sees Noah's car. In his frantic state, Darius questions nothing and jumps into the back seat.

"Where to?" Noah asks, ignoring the blood that covers Darius's hands and face. Noah's demeanor remains unexpectedly … jolly.

"I don't know where to go," Darius admits, but then he blurts, "To Quiet End!"

"Whatever you say."

As Noah maneuvers through Zalmon's morning traffic, Darius activates his phone. It displays his customary options:

Phone Mom?

Phone Mahlah?

Phone Zuriel?

Phone Vocation Office?

Phone Medical Center?

Darius feels a dagger to his heart, noticing for the first time that the Communications Center has wiped *Phone Grandpa Felix* from the list. Why? He's not even dead yet. He's still awaiting his Welcome Release at Quiet End.

But alas, Darius has to make a choice, and he does. He selects the third option.

"Darius?" Zuriel answers.

Noah listens in on Darius's end of the conversation.

"You busy?" Darius asks Zuriel.

"Yes. I'm just about to assist with a Release."

"I … I need … someone." Darius rubs his eyes.

"What for? I can't see you right now."

"Can I meet you there?" Darius presses.

Noah eyes Darius in the rearview mirror.

"You know the rules, Darius," Zuriel answers.

"I'll slip in the back. No one will know." He hangs up the phone before Zuriel can protest.

Noah pulls the car up to the unassuming rear door of Quiet End. Darius reads its signage: Shipping and Receiving.

Before Noah releases the car doors, he turns to Darius in the back seat and hands him a small paper.

"For in case you need that hand looked after," Noah says.

Darius is suddenly aware of his blood-soaked knuckles. He looks down at them. He looks over at the paper. He looks into Noah's eyes and swears he can see his reflection in them. Darius takes the paper. He runs his finger over a small, bizarre, snake-like symbol embossed in its corner alongside the name *Aysa Relenday*.

"Off you go." Noah releases the car door locks.

Darius sneaks through the long, desolate hallways of Quiet End before he finds his way to a massive, bright-white room. He sees a small table with the Book on it and a big, uncomfortable-looking chair. To the left, he sees a closet. Darius enters the closet to hide. He closes the door tight.

Zuriel enters the room, pushing a cart full of strange apparatuses. She is with a woman in her forties who wears her hair slicked back in a bun and balances thin-rimmed wire glasses near the tip of her nose.

Zuriel mirrors all of the woman's moves. When the woman walks over to a cabinet, Zuriel walks over to the cabinet. When the woman puts on latex gloves, Zuriel puts on latex gloves.

Not far behind the two of them is a man in his late fifties. The man is slightly overweight and dressed from head to toe in baby-soft white cotton pajamas.

The woman turns around to greet the man. "Oh, Mr. Sheba. You look very nice."

Zuriel hands a tall glass to Mr. Sheba. He takes a long, slow drink. His hands tremble.

"Mr. Sheba, that is Zuriel," the woman announces. "Zuriel is my apprentice."

"My wishes." Zuriel curtsies slightly as she's introduced.

"Hello," Mr. Sheba manages.

"Zuriel is going to walk you over to that chair and settle you in," the woman says.

Mr. Sheba peers at the chair as unruly tears glaze his eyes. The peace that he once felt about his Final Days abandons him now.

"Now now, Mr. Sheba, there's nothing to cry about." The woman purses her lips. "This is your Welcome Release," she reminds him. "Rejoice."

The man nods.

The woman motions for Zuriel to get *The Book of Zalmon.* Zuriel practically trips, she's so excited. She grabs the Book in one hand, then she approaches the man and double-taps his arm with her other. Zuriel's initiative makes the woman smile. To reward her pupil, she starts to leave the room.

"Really?" Zuriel beams.

"I've never been more confident that things are under control," the woman says, intent on a longer lunch break.

"You're not going to be here?" Mr. Sheba worries. "She's so young and —"

"Would you like me to read to you, Mr. Sheba?" Zuriel asks.

The man watches the woman leave the room. His breaths are shallow. Resignedly, he nods.

In the closet, Darius wonders if he should pop out. He can't see what's going on from here, but he can definitely sense the gravity of the moment.

Zuriel opens the Book, parts her blood-red, lipsticked lips, licks her finger, and flips to a dog-eared page. She bows her head for a moment of silence before she reads aloud.

"Our Welcome Release is the epitome of all grand days. The day we arrange to be at one with our Master. The day for which we lived our lives wholly, submissively, and obediently." Zuriel extends her hand and points a finger at Mr. Sheba. "We praise those who embrace the final moments of this life in Zalmon, knowing of the blessed eternity thereafter." She turns the page. "We are not here simply because we fear a Natural Death. We are here to revel blissfully in the Zalmon promise."

Mr. Sheba wipes tears from his cheeks. Oblivious, Zuriel closes the Book and returns it to the table. She looks up and smiles at Mr. Sheba, then she leads him to the chair.

Darius doesn't know what in the world is going on out there now. It's quiet. Too quiet. He wants out. He opens the door slightly to assess the situation. He sees that both Zuriel and the man have their full attention on the chair, and he opens the door fully, slinks along the wall, and narrowly escapes the room.

Darius knows that trespassing into Quiet End is punishable. Although they entertain anyone who books guided tours and Final Visits, absolutely no one is permitted to run the grounds unattended and purposeless. Darius keeps out of sight of personnel as he moves in and out of hidden corners and empty corridors. Once he enters the familiar communal areas, he stays guarded and makes his way to the painting room. He peeks inside. It's empty; he was hoping to find his grandfather in there.

Someone is coming. Darius hides behind the painting room door. Through the crack, Darius sees Priya. She takes his breath away as she wanders around the room from station to station, putting away paintbrushes and straightening splattered easels.

Priya stops at one of the easels and looks over her shoulder, making sure she's in the clear before picking up a paintbrush. She smiles a smile to herself that warms Darius from head to toe. He tiptoes up to her quietly.

Priya dips the paintbrush into a leftover yellow mixture and makes a nearly perfect circle in the middle of a small, incomplete canvas. As she fills in the shape, she sways her hips in time with the brush strokes, mesmerized by the symphony it yields in her mind.

"Hi," Darius whispers.

Priya gasps and bumps into the easel, tipping it onto her thighs. A rainbow of vibrant colors soaks the front of her soft pink uniform. She flurries to clean it up.

"What are you doing here, Darius?" she whisper-yells.

"Please don't tell anyone. I'll be out in a minute. I just need to know where my grandfather is."

Priya avoids eye contact.

Darius dips his head to catch her eyes. There is a long pause. Too long. Darius knows what it means.

"When?"

"Last week," she mumbles. "I'm sorry, Darius. I thought you knew."

Darius wants to erupt, but something about Priya's apologetic voice calms him. "No. I didn't know. I can't believe he went even earlier than early. I was hoping he'd change his mind and come home."

"Oh, Darius, no one chooses a Natural —"

"Please. Do not go there," Darius says.

"Felix talked a lot about your dad."

Darius glares at her. He wants to tell her everything about Mahlah and how she averted a Natural Death or whatever in the world transpired last night, but he knows he can't. Or shouldn't.

"I wanted my grandfather to spend his final weeks with us," he says.

"Well, he really wanted to be with his Rhonda." Priya looks around, then whispers, "I probably shouldn't say this; it won't make you feel better, but ... he did say that he was very lonely here."

"Why didn't he call us?"

Suddenly, a voice from the doorway chills them. "It was forbidden."

Zuriel.

"You already had your Final Visit with him," she says. She eyes the colorful spill on Priya's uniform.

Priya whips around and tends to the easels and cleanup duty.

Zuriel turns to Darius. "Felix is at peace."

"Nice of you to tell me."

"You said you needed me, Darius?" Zuriel emphasizes it loud and proud as Priya pretends not to hear.

Darius grabs Zuriel's arm and yanks her out of the painting room.

〜

Back outside, near the Shipping and Receiving door, Darius finally lets go of Zuriel. She rubs the spot left in place of his hand.

"What are you thinking, grabbing me like that?" Zuriel is disgusted. "Anyone could have caught us in there!"

"There's a lot of shit going on, Zuriel. I have questions."

"You always have questions," Zuriel says, rolling her eyes.

Darius starts to respond but is distracted by the sight of Noah driving oddly around the parking lot.

"Seriously, Darius," Zuriel pushes. "You're just like your father."

Darius clenches his fists. He doesn't know what to do with the anger inside of him. He howls and punches the wall repeatedly. He likes the hurt.

"I'll report you if you don't pull yourself together," Zuriel threatens. "They'll detain you for Relationship Intervention counseling. Say bye-bye to your weekends, dear." With a huff, she retreats inside.

As Darius pounds the pavement, he becomes aware that Noah is following him in his car. "You can trust me, kid," Noah calls out through an open window. "Get in."

DRIVE

Darius has been in the back seat of many Zalmon cars. He has casually met the eyes of many Zalmon drivers. But he senses there is something different going on right now. He can't quite put his finger on it, but he's taken aback by a spark in Noah's eyes, and he feels the fire in Noah's exhale.

"Talk to me, kid." Noah's voice slices through the thick air between them. "You're safe."

Safe? The empty word mocks Darius, who just glares out the window. Who does this guy think he is?

"I know that look, kid. I know you know something."

Darius hesitates before he blurts, "My sister's ... my little sister ... there's just ... something wrong with my sister." Sweat pools in his palms.

"That's it?" Noah asks. "There's just something wrong with your sister?"

Darius smashes his hands into the upholstery of the passenger seat, sending it flying forward.

"What do you mean that's it?" he yells. "Isn't that enough?"

Noah hides a smirk.

"What do you want?" Darius loses it. "You want her dead like everyone else?"

Noah turns left sharply, flinging Darius to the other side of the car and cutting his head on the half-open window.

"What are you doing?" Darius shouts.

Noah ignores him.

"Where do you think you're going?"

Still nothing.

"This is not the way to my house, asshole." Darius tries to open his door, despite the neck-breaking speed, but the childproof lock imprisons him.

Noah pounds the gas pedal to the metal. The car burns rubber, expelling clouds of smoke into the Zalmon air.

"I said, where are you going?!"

"Just trust me, kid." Noah concentrates like a jacked-up mouse in a maze, intent on the cheese.

"Trust you?" Darius laughs. "I don't even know you."

Noah musters more speed and whips past the last row of Zalmon's houses.

Darius kicks at his door handle. "You're crazy! Let me out of here before I rip your fucking face off."

Their car flies past billboards of tight-knit nuclear families, feet cushioned in plastic grass, homes enclosed by white picket fences. Darius jerks his head to watch the signs of civilization diminish out the back window.

Noah laughs through one last wild turn, then his car flies over the hump of the paved road's end and halts on a dirt road.

Darius has never been here before, but he's heard of this spot. It's the complete opposite point of the Zalmon border, known as the Edge of Town. It's as boring as they all say. All Darius can see is a massive, thick forest. Darius and all Zalmon kids are taught, at a very young, impressionable age, that beyond the darkness of the forest is a deep, wide body of water where Leavers lose their lives to the vicious, engulfing waves.

Noah does a three-point turn. Just as Darius works up the nerve to jump into the front seat and try the door, Noah pulls the gear shift down, cranks the gas, and guns it directly into the sprawling trees.

"Please stop!" Darius yells.

Baby trees bend and bow in sync with the racing car. Branches thrash at the windows. Leaves are long streaks of blurred green.

Noah doesn't let up. He speeds right on through until he reaches a hidden, dark mud tunnel and rips the vehicle masterfully into the tight opening. Noah accelerates, then cuts the lights to maneuver the rest of the way by memory.

Darius jumps back into the back seat and heaves.

A small light shines in the distance, casting a soft glow onto Noah's closed eyelids.

From behind, Darius reaches his hands up and wraps them around Noah's throat.

Noah opens his eyes and slams on the brakes. The car swerves, just missing the sides of the tunnel. Darius squeezes Noah's throat harder. The car skids to the other side of the tunnel, scrapes it, and spins around. Darius's hands close tighter yet. Noah slowly loses consciousness as the light at the end of the tunnel draws nearer. The car slows to a stop just as Noah's breathing does.

The driver's side door flies open at the hands of Aysa Relenday, a man in his mid-forties with deceptive strength. Despite Darius's constrictive hold on Noah's throat, the calm, tattooed, and goateed Aysa frees Noah with one knockout punch to Darius's chin.

DIG

In the dark, damp Underground, Darius comes to. He's bound to a chair by rugged leather straps. His injured hand is bandaged, and he has an elastic tourniquet around his bicep, restricting blood flow.

Darius wonders what the f—

"There are traces of Seroquel in you," Aysa says as he stands tall in front of Darius. Aysa's bald head glistens. A jagged scar in the shape of an L rests above his eyebrow. Expertly, he loosens the tourniquet from Darius's arm.

"Seroquel?" Darius's mouth is so dry, he can barely form the word.

"But someone obviously missed a few of his doses, ain't that right?" Aysa laughs. Another laugh echoes his from the corner. Darius looks over at the oldest man he's ever seen.

"That's Jir. A treasure. Just look at him," Aysa says.

Darius couldn't even guess his age — he's wrinkly all over, and his hair is bright white. He sits with a tube tucked into his nostrils. It's plugged into what looks like a tank.

"Don't worry about him."

Darius looks back at Aysa. "I don't know what Sero—"

"You know it as an Abater." Aysa laughs some more. So does the ancient guy.

Darius scans the small room. It isn't well-lit — it has only one loosely wired bulb hanging from the middle of the clay ceiling. Darius notices his opened wallet on a lopsided table in the far corner.

The thick, dried mud walls smother Darius. There are no windows, and the ceiling is low. And Aysa scares the shit out of him.

"I only take them when I need to." Darius works his way back to the topic of conversation.

"So, tell me a little bit about yourself, Darius." Aysa seems past it; he folds his massive arms.

Darius wonders how this man knows his name, but then he remembers his wallet.

Darius has heard about the Underground through secret rumblings his whole life, but like some mythical concoction, he never once believed it was real. He always thought that if it did exist, he, of all people, would be privy to it.

Is this actually a room in the hidden, seedy place where out-laws gather secretly to frolic in Zalmon's forbidden pleasures?

Darius surveys the piles of books everywhere. He considers himself very well-read — it is his chosen pastime, and he knows every single book in his school library — but these are all titles he's never once heard of. He makes out the words on some of their spines: *Maus, Lawn Boy, Out of Darkness, The Bluest Eye, Harry Potter, The Handmaid's Tale …*

"Those aren't Zalmon books," Darius says.

"Oh, you've read all the books, have you?" Aysa snorts.

"Yes."

Aysa clears his throat. "No, they aren't. They're randoms found at the Edge."

"From regretful Leavers?"

"Any other explanation?"

A noise just beyond the room distracts Darius. He looks over at the closed door and tries desperately to make out the sounds; however, they're conquered by heavy music that mocks the weak solos of Zalmon's only classical music options.

Darius wonders, if this is the Underground, how does it function? Why hasn't it been discovered by the government?

"Where the f—?"

"Stop playing games, would you? You know where you are." There's something in the way Aysa says this that shuts Darius up. "And you'll keep this unicorn sighting to yourself," Aysa continues. "We take things very seriously down here."

"Ain't that the truth," his sidekick pipes up.

"Darius, I'm sure I'll like you, eventually," Aysa says, "but right now, I don't. And I'm known to be a really impulsive son of a bitch, if you get what I'm saying." Aysa steps aside to reveal an unstable bookshelf of loaded syringes and small bottles of pills in different colors from any he's ever seen. Small, sharp scalpels catch light on their edges.

"Yep. I can kill you," Aysa adds for effect.

Darius clears his throat.

∽

Darius rubs the raw indent on his bicep from the tourniquet as he walks alongside Aysa, led only by a fire-breathing lantern through the cave-like, makeshift corridors.

"You're not eighteen, so when I say to avert your eyes, avert your eyes," Aysa commands.

"I'm practically eighteen." Darius stands straighter.

"When I say to avert your eyes, avert your eyes."

"In the Underground?" Darius laughs. "I thought nothing was sacred down here —"

Aysa slams Darius against the cold wall, avalanching bits of clay onto his shoulders.

"Everything down here is sacred, kid," Aysa manages through clenched teeth. "You've got it all wrong, you little punk. We honor what happens in these walls; you understand?"

Darius nods.

The blackness of Aysa's eyes relents as he lightens his grip.

"You're still a kid, Darius. I'm not into poisoning the impressionable minds of our youth, unlike our leaders. But, come adulthood, fair is fair." Aysa laughs. "You're lucky Noah convinced me to let you down here to take a peek."

Darius looks around for Noah, who is nowhere to be found.

As the two round a corner that opens up into massive, dug-out pods, Aysa gestures with a sweeping hand and bellows, "Welcome to the Underground."

They stand before a gathering of people, feet up and surrounded by clouds of oddly scented smoke. Darius doesn't recognize the smell but takes it in. An extraordinarily long-haired woman raises a strange, stemmed glass and nods slowly to Darius before she gulps down the last of whatever maroon liquid she was drinking. Darius notes the woman's arms. They look like someone took thin, black markers and drew all over them. Darius makes out the shape of roses (which he's only seen at Quiet End), a skull like the one he's seen on posters in his doctor's office, and an image similar to what Darius imagines a "dog" would look like if they really existed beyond a few books he's read.

Aysa leads Darius to another pod, where there is a spread of strange foods unlike anything Darius has ever seen. The colors and textures are so different from the fruits, vegetables, and simple nourishment he's known his whole life. Some of the foods look like birthday once-a-year treats, but brighter and cut into little pyramids.

Aysa watches as Darius runs his fingers along the edges of the goodies. Without asking, Darius dips a finger into a whipped topping then places some of it on the tip of his tongue. Intense flavor erupts in his mouth. Eager for more, he breaks a small chunk from the corner of one of the milky-brown rectangular prisms. The velvety sweetness blankets his tongue. His pleasure is audible.

"Chocolate," Aysa informs him. He pulls Darius out of the pod, but not before Darius jams a fistful of the chocolates into his pockets.

Around the corner, the vibrations of musical beats thump Darius's soul. The notes harmonize with his pulse; energy surges into his hips, shoulders, and toes. It takes all the control Darius can muster to not move to the sounds, unlike all of the people he watches groove before him. Their bodies twist and contort in time with the music. Their smiles beam in the flecks of light reflected from a spinning mirror ball hanging mid-ceiling.

Tucked way back, far in the twisting and narrowing hallways, is a pod with its door open only a crack. Darius stops and peeks in.

"Not on my watch, kid. You're underage," Aysa reminds him. But there's something about this kid that disarms Aysa. "Thirty seconds," he sighs. "No more." Aysa starts a timer on his watch.

Darius gawks at people engaged in the kind of forbidden body contact he's only ever dreamed of. Clothes hang scantily from stunning women, revealing their breasts and rear ends. Hands caress and grope. Mouths open and press. Bodies hover and dip. The smell of sweat swirls through the air. Hard breaths and moans synchronize then alternate like an orchestra of sirens.

"Time's up." Aysa pulls the collar of Darius's shirt and yanks him away.

Darius stares at shelves upon shelves of urine samples in this new room. He knows exactly what they are because every few years, the doctor's office requires specimens from every citizen. Darius feels like a fish in some strange, yellow-watered aquarium.

"We switch them out as necessary," Aysa says.

"Switch them out?" Darius echoes.

"We're not exactly pure down here." Aysa laughs. "But we sure know how to fake it."

Darius turns to the rows of supplies at the back of the room and notes their likeness to the ones he's seen in his doctor's office: cotton balls, a blood pressure machine, tongue depressors, and some weird steel apparatus at the foot of the bed that looks like it would suspend his feet up in the air.

Aysa reads Darius's mind. "It's like a hospital."

Darius is confused. "What's a … hospital?"

"It's where sick people should get treated."

Darius tries to process that.

Aysa pulls up a chair right in front of Darius. He plops himself into it and leans forward. "Noah tells me your sister's sick," he whispers. "I want to help."

"She's not sick, she's —"

"She's sick."

"No, it's just that she was supposed to get a Death Date Card, but —"

"Sick, Darius."

Darius can feel the heat in his face. What does this guy mean? "She's not Datura," he says.

"She's sick." Aysa is relentless. "And I want to help her."

"You want to help her?" Darius laughs. "Why?"

"Because I'm a doctor."

Darius lets that sink in for a moment. "You're telling me she's not Datura, but something is … wrong?"

"And it's not short-term." Aysa smiles. Darius wants to smack it off his face.

Darius is so bent out of shape that he can't put anything into words.

"I need you to get a hold of your sister's Annuals data," Aysa says. "I need to know what they've got on her. Think you can handle that, punk?"

STEAL

Darius tries to close the open back of his medical gown. His butt cheeks goosebump in the breezy doctor's office. He fiddles his thumbs as he sits on the edge of the bed and waits for his doctor.

Darius isn't pleased to be in this situation. One minute he's in the Underground, the next, he's brainwashed into thinking that sickness exists and "doctor" Aysa needs Mahlah's paperwork to prove it.

Darius believes Mahlah is perfect. There is absolutely nothing wrong with her — the system must have just messed up with a Death Date.

The doctor comes into the small examination room. He glances over his clipboard notes and then eyes Darius. *Oh great, another Anah kid.*

"You made an appointment, Darius?"

"Yes."

The doctor isn't at his most patient. "And?" he presses. "What seems to be the problem?"

"I'm feeling more … aggressive these days." Darius clenches his fists for added effect. Sicknesses of the mind are the only true things that Darius knows of that he can fake.

The doctor stares blankly at Darius. "Self-diagnosed defiance? It doesn't measure up." He shakes his head. "You know, Darius, time in this room is a precious commodity. Zalmon prides itself on every person's unequivocal right to quick and reliable medical attention, but —"

"'But shall not congest its offerings with puerile matters of insignificance.' I know, Doc, I know. I agree to the terms every time I book an appointment." Darius shuffles. His gown frees more ass cheek. "I just don't feel right."

"Your records show adequate hormone levels."

Darius doesn't know what *hormone* means. Before he can clarify, the doctor continues.

"Your Abaters are working just fine."

"I tried to kill my mother," Darius lies. He raises his bandaged hand for effect.

The doctor studies him then jots a note on his papers. "I'll have to discuss the matter with my … mentor." He rubs the small bump behind his ear. "Please sit tight and give me a few minutes."

The doctor leaves. Darius smirks, stands up, holds the back of his gown closed, and tiptoes into the hallway. He notes the way the doctor turned then darts in the opposite direction.

In the file room, Darius rummages through a long row of stuffed manila folders searching for one with the name *Anah*. He grows impatient with the seemingly infinite array. High-heeled feet approach and break his concentration. His fingers flick through tabs at warp speed.

The door handle turns, and the door starts to open …

Darius throws his foot against the door and slams it back shut. The office assistant huffs and turns the handle incessantly. Darius locks the deadbolt.

The woman knocks. "What's going on in there?"

Near the very end of the cabinet, Darius finally finds Mahlah's file and tears it from its squished spot.

Another knock.

"Let me in." The assistant's voice cracks.

Darius tucks Mahlah's folder under his medical gown and holds it tight against his belly. He whips open the back of his gown, unlocks the door, and falls forward.

The woman flies into the room.

Mostly naked, Darius shocks her silly.

"What in the world!" she shouts.

"I need a bathroom, please!" Darius rocks back and forth, his back arched and buttocks high and mighty.

"Please! Please get up," the assistant begs him. "You should not be in here!"

"I'm going to crap myself!"

"This is not the bathroom!"

"I know that! But at least it's private! I'm not going to make it! Get out!"

"No! Let me go get you something! Just … hold on!"

As soon as the assistant is out of sight, Darius whips upright, secures the hidden folder, and rushes back into his doctor's room as if nothing ever happened.

⌐~

The Underground bustles with rebels, but Darius is focused on Aysa, who sits in front of him, holding Mahlah's records on his lap.

"How'd you get these?" Aysa asks.

"It's moot. Nothing an ass couldn't do." Only he gets the joke.

"We need to talk about something," Aysa says. "Noah tells me that your sister's Death Date ... passed?"

"Yes," Darius confirms.

"Yet she didn't check in to Quiet End?" Aysa scratches his bald head.

"She didn't even know about it."

"Stop being cryptic, punk!"

"No one knew, okay!" Darius shouts. "No one knows. I broke into the system just to cause shit, and I came across her Death Date. I ... deleted it."

"You what?" Aysa leans in.

"I didn't want her to go there to die."

"You got balls, kid." He takes another look at Mahlah's records. "I mean, I hate a lot of things, and I stand up to a shitload, but you ... you knew you'd be exposing your baby sister to a Natural Death, and you still went ahead with it." He bursts out laughing. "That's pretty messed up."

"I wanted to be with her when it happened."

"What's life like living just for you, Darius?" Aysa chuckles.

Darius stands up and rips the folder from Aysa's hands. "Fuck you." He turns to storm out of the room.

Aysa grabs Darius by the shoulders and heaves him back into a chair like a sack of potatoes. "Sit down, you little prick!"

Darius nurses his shoulders.

Aysa claws Mahlah's folder back and sits down. He opens it and flips through the papers before he stops at one in particular. He looks up at Darius. "Says here your dad's a Leaver and your mom's Datura."

"Yep." Darius snickers. "Does that explain me for you?"

Aysa pauses. "Well, I'm sorry about your dad. We accept a lot of things down here, but even we don't condone Leavers. Cowardly creeps. And unfortunately, I can't do much about your mom — I never once treated a Datura. None ever find their way down here. I've tried to approach them countless times, and they run away from me the second I start talking —"

Aysa pauses as something on the paper strikes him.

"Says here that your mom has a Second Match. Now, that's very rare for a Datura. She must be exceptional."

That makes Darius laugh. "There's nothing rare ... nothing special about her. At all. She's just an everyday, useless, piece-of-shit Datura."

"So who's her Second Match? It's not listed here where it usually is."

"Why? What does it matter?" Darius strikes out.

"I ask questions when things are odd." Aysa is surprisingly patient. "Who is the Second Match?"

"My stupid manager. Abram Job. Walks like he has a pickle up his ass. Loser in a fancy suit all the time. He's a nobody."

"A nobody who gets to fiddle your mom."

Darius holds back his reaction.

Aysa closes Mahlah's folder and hands it back to Darius.

"As for your sister, here's the deal. Her body can't produce enough of a thing called a hormone —"

There's that word again. Darius still doesn't understand it.

"Specifically insulin. She has terminal blood sugar levels."

Darius is confused by the word *terminal*. The only definition he knows is related to driving and the parking lots.

"What do you mean?"

"I've seen something like this in a few of the much older junk-eaters around here," Aysa continues. "But someone this young?" He shakes his head. "She will certainly die a Natural Death if something isn't done quick."

Darius is incredulous. "Wait a minute. Something can be done?"

"I think so," Aysa says.

Darius bolts up. "You're telling me that something can be done to make Mahlah better?"

"I'm telling you I think so. This isn't my area of —"

"Then why is no one doing anything already?" Darius picks up his chair and throws it against the shelves. The urine samples smash to the ground, and the pungent smell fills the room.

Calmly, Aysa retrieves Darius's chair, places it upright, and motions for him to sit back down. Darius does.

"You're not going to like the sounds of this," Aysa begins. "Zalmon prioritizes money over people. Although in all my years, I've never once imagined they'd stoop so low as to dispose of a little girl."

CONFIDE

At Quiet End, Darius hides behind a shining white, granite, unbreakable wall.

Priya is done her shift. She pulls a light jacket over her pink uniform and whips her long hair into a messy bun. She's wiped. Once she clears the main reception area, she closes the Employees Only door behind her and tucks her security card back into her bra.

As she heads for the drivers' parking lot, Darius pounces from behind the wall. Priya jumps straight off the ground and barely contains a screech.

"Stop scaring me," she manages.

Darius takes Priya's hand and tows her into his hiding spot then pulls Mahlah's file from under his coat.

Priya looks down at the papers that protrude from the folder and points to a red one. "Closing Annual file?"

"You know that?" Darius shakes his head.

"So many of these come through here at work. I stamp the Release dates."

"Priya, you have to stop working here."

"Why does it bother you so much, Darius?" She peers into his eyes, tugging at his soul.

Hunched between vacant cars parked way at the back of the lot, Priya buries her head in her hands. Remnants of fallen tears stain her cheeks, crystallized as streaks of salt. She looks up at a rare gray bird, nestled high in one of the fake trees. Not even it can distract her from the matter at hand: the knowledge of the Underground.

"But it doesn't make sense, Darius," she manages. "None of what you just said makes any sense."

"Apparently Mahlah is … expendable," Darius says.

"What does that mean, though?"

"To them—whoever *they* are—Mahlah would cost Zalmon more than she's worth."

"It's absurd," Priya blurts. "If they could help her, if there were any way they could make her life longer, they would. She's a little girl! She's an incredible little girl!" Priya cries.

In that instant, Darius is sure he's never liked Priya more.

"I think everything I told you is true, Priya. Very few people know it. Fewer believe it. I don't blame your atheism."

"I think I'm going to be sick." Priya places her hand on Darius's forearm for stability. When the nausea passes, rather than retract her hand, she looks around to make sure no one sees it.

Darius slowly puts his other hand on top of Priya's. He rubs his thumb over the hills and valleys of her knuckles then dips it into her palm. It tickles Priya. For a brief moment, the two of them are lost in forbidden thoughts.

Priya snaps to. "Darius, why did you tell me all of this?"

He pauses. For a split second he considers spilling the beans about his deep respect and trust for her. He yearns to tell her how he feels disobediently drawn to her, despite the revelations of his Cards.

"Because of your Vocation Position," he says instead. "You're pre-doc, and I need your help."

"Get Zuriel's help."

Darius ignores the suggestion and reaches into his pocket. He opens up a crumpled paper bag.

"I need you to show Mahlah how to use this." Darius holds a syringe and a small glass vial marked *Insulin*.

Priya is taken aback. "I'm only mid-theory. I —"

"Without this, she'll die, Priya," Darius pleads.

"Who says? Some freak from the Underground?"

"He's a doctor," Darius assures her.

"He's a liar. I don't know what's going on. Maybe he's got some sick sense of humor. Maybe he's trying to impress you so you don't take him for the loser he is." Priya stands up. "I know all of the doctors in Zalmon, Darius. They're at the office, or they're at Quiet End doing Final Checks and Post-Assessments. That's it. They don't hide out in clay tunnels and watch people practice procreation all day!"

"I'm telling you, she will die!" Darius shouts.

"Well, maybe. So what, Darius? We all will. Maybe it's a lovely thing."

"Now you're sounding like my Life Match," Darius jabs.

Priya starts to walk away.

Darius follows her. "Listen, I can understand how you'd be duped into thinking a Welcome Release is beautiful for oldies, but Mahlah? She's a kid! An incredible kid. You literally just said —"

Priya whips around. "Duped? Do you think I'm stupid, Darius?"

She's the smartest person he knows, but that isn't the point.

"You?" Priya points at him. "A guy who trusts no one, yet you trust this random guy with your sister's life?"

"He's the only one, Priya! No one's knocking down my door to do a damn thing about me losing the most important person in my world."

She shakes her head. "I can't do it Darius. But maybe I can talk to some of the real doctors for you. And you should talk to Zuriel!"

"Are you crazy?!" Darius yells. "You cannot tell a soul, Priya." Darius bleeds desperation in a vulnerable look. "Please," he begs.

"Okay, fine — I won't. But you can and should tell Zuriel. She's your Life Match. You have an 'immortal bond that outshines, overpowers, and outlasts all' —"

"Spare me the words of the Book, Priya. I thought you were different."

They both take a moment to compose themselves.

"I'm sorry," Priya says. "I'm just … I'm scared Darius. When I'm scared, I don't know what to do."

"I call bullshit," Darius declares. "I think you do know what to do."

Priya shakes her head again. "Listen, Darius —"

He puts the syringe and the vial back into the paper bag then shoves them all into his pocket. "I have to go," he says. "I have to work."

Darius begins to walk away, then he looks back and says, "I know I will see you later, at my house."

Priya shakes her head harder. She calls after him. "Darius!"

He runs off.

There is a knock on the side of Abram's cubicle as he sits at his desk, pretending to be the manager of this electrical usage monitoring and data processing company. He shuffles a prop stack of papers and removes his feet from the edge of his desk before he looks over his shoulder.

Darius walks into the small space. Abram holds up his index finger to request another second. He pretends to finish typing a message and reads aloud, "I feel you should cut them some slack. Proceed to sign off on their custodial labor disputes immediately." He hits a final key. "Ah, Darius."

"You wanted to see me?"

"What happened to your hand?"

Darius eyes his bandaged hand. "This hand?" he asks. "How'd you know about it?"

"I saw you favoring it out there."

"I punched a door."

Abram looks at him knowingly. Darius misses it.

"You know, Darius, you're a snarky kid. But I'm a rock. Unlike some people in your life, I would never Leave on account of your behavior."

Darius shrugs off the dig at him and his father. He knows Abram is trying to get a reaction. "What's that got to do with anything?"

"It means that nothing you could say to me would make me

go away. As you know, I'm not only your boss" — Abram smiles — "I'm practically part of your family."

Darius glances into Abram's eyes, then looks away. He thinks for a second about what Aysa said. Why *is* Abram his mother's Second Match? How did that happen?

Abram interrupts Darius's thoughts. "A real man knows when another … almost-man is in turmoil. You seem conflicted these days, and your mother is concerned."

"Ha!"

"It's true, Darius. She talks to me about it all the time."

"That's really great that she talks to you all the time. She's healed!"

"I'm going to let that slide. I see right past your guise of disrespect, my friend." Abram smiles.

Darius wonders if Abram has nothing better to do than piss him off. But maybe Priya was right. Maybe someone can help him with Mahlah's situation. Maybe that someone is Abram. Darius shuffles his feet.

"It's Mahlah," he opens up. "She's … sick. Like, not an emotional sick, but sick sick."

Abram was not expecting to hear that. He thought possibly Darius would divulge his knowledge about Mahlah's Death Date interruption, but never in a million years did he anticipate Darius would know about Mahlah's illness.

"What do you mean?" Abram plays dumb and holds it together while his blood boils and his eyes want to pop out of their sockets.

But Darius senses the intensity in Abram's voice. His question is void of concern and lacks disbelief. Darius wants to go into detail about Mahlah's illness and yearns to trust his mother's

Match, but Abram's reaction makes Darius uncomfortable. He proceeds with caution.

"Like, she's really shaky. She's pissing a lot, and she can't sleep." Darius sticks to Mahlah's outward signs — signs he thinks his mother would have mentioned to her Second Match anyway. He's very careful not to share anything from Mahlah's files and steers dead away from his conversations with Aysa. "I just can't think of any other word for it other than sick."

"That's it?" Abram leans in.

"What do you mean?" Darius asks.

"That's all you know?" Abram clarifies.

Darius looks deep into Abram's eyes. Abram stares back.

"I, uh, better get back to work." Darius backs up. "I started late and all."

He turns and walks away from Abram's cubicle.

INJECT

It's pitch-dark outside. Priya paces out front of Darius's house. She questions what she's doing there. She questions her integrity, her oath as a citizen of Zalmon, her decision-making skills, her lack of resilience, and above all, why it's so hard to say no to Darius Anah.

Priya looks over her shoulder, not only to see if anyone is watching her but also to gauge how far away the closest driver is in case she wants to bail.

Okay, she wants to bail.

She turns around to summon a driver —

But she's stopped by the sound of Darius's voice.

"Priya, wait!"

Priya hesitates, but then turns around. She eyes Darius in his doorway. She watches as his expression of fear morphs into a glimmer of hope at the mere sight of … her. She warms from head to toe. She knows she cannot let Darius down.

Priya jogs up the pathway. She's never been here before. She's forbidden to visit on account of having no official business at the home. But with each step, her sense of purpose grows.

Darius isn't sure how to communicate his relief at Priya's presence. All he can muster is, "What took you so long?"

Priya steps up onto his porch.

"She's bad, Priya. Mahlah's really bad."

The two of them rush into the house and up the stairs.

In her bedroom, Mahlah paces from one end of the room to the other as she mumbles incessantly, barely audible, to no one in particular.

Priya and Darius tear in.

Priya tries to approach, but Mahlah won't have it. She acts as if she's possessed. Scared, Priya steps backward.

"Where's your mother?" Priya asks Darius.

Mahlah throws a ceramic pencil holder that just misses Priya's head.

"Leave me alone!" Mahlah yells as she succumbs to whole-body tremors. Darius grabs his sister to calm her, but she jumps at his touch and retreats to the far corner of her room.

Darius turns to Priya. "She's absolutely freezing," he says. "Please hurry up."

Darius tosses Priya the brown paper bag with the insulin and syringe.

Mahlah spots the needle as Priya opens the bag.

"What is that? No, no, no, no, no, no, no, no …" She twists and wiggles, contained to the corner; Darius approaches her slowly. His hands reach out ahead of him to coerce her into submission. Mahlah grabs her head and rocks it to and fro wildly, heightening her state of confusion. Darius pounces on her and restrains her.

To Darius's surprise, Mahlah stops suddenly. Her eyes pierce her brother's. Her intense gaze darkens as she questions him. "Who are you?"

Darius swallows hard, holds Mahlah tighter yet, then yells at Priya, "Hurry up!"

Priya fumbles the needle; it drops to the floor, barely missing her big toe. She bends down to pick it up with her shaking fingers.

"Didn't you say we have to check her levels first?" Priya yells back at Darius.

"Look at her, Priya! It's obvious! We don't have time. Just do it!"

Mahlah musters an incredible fight against Darius. She turns to him and punches him over and over with inconceivable, painful strength. Darius isn't sure how to stop her. He tries to hold her arms still, to no avail. Mahlah's jabs are animalistic.

Downstairs, the front door opens. Sela walks in holding a grocery bag filled to the brim with fruits and vegetables. She drops her house key on a small table and stops dead at the sound of the commotion upstairs.

A surge of fight overtakes Darius. He wrestles his little sister down and pins her to the floor. Darius has her in a bear hug, and Mahlah is finally still enough for Priya to administer the medication. Priya stands over them, loaded syringe in hand, but —

Sweat loosens her grip, and she drops it again.

"Do it now!" Darius screams.

"I've only watched them use syringes, Darius! I've never used one myself!" Priya cries as she squirts a bit of liquid out of the syringe. She raises her hand high and tries to steady it directly above Mahlah.

Sela hovers just outside of Mahlah's room. She holds one hand over her mouth in shock while her other is airtight below her ear.

Mahlah jerks violently in Darius's arms. He struggles to hold up her T-shirt to expose her belly for the shot.

Priya cries harder. "You do it, Darius! I can't!"

"I can't!" Darius screams back. "I'm holding her with all I've got!"

Priya is dumbfounded.

"Mahlah's going to die, damn it!" Darius wails.

Sela bursts into the room, shrieking at the top of her lungs.

Priya and Darius whip around at her entrance.

Mahlah's convulsions consume her.

"Mom! Get out of here!" Darius hollers.

Mahlah barks absurdities.

Sela studies her spasming daughter, on the floor in her son's arms. Then she surveys the insulin bottle and syringe in Priya's hands.

Sela runs across the room, rips the syringe from Priya's hand, and drives it into her daughter's skin.

Priya backs all the way back into a corner.

Darius holds Mahlah tight until she grows heavy in his arms and passes out.

Sela shakes her head at Darius.

"What are you shaking your head for?" Darius asks. "I tried to tell you she was sick!"

Sela holds her hand over her ear again and whispers, "Be quiet, Darius!"

"Don't worry your pretty little head anymore, Mom. She'll be fine. I got her these meds —"

Sela drowns out Darius's words with incoherent screams as she waves her hands about.

Priya shields her eyes. Darius notices and shouts, "Don't embarrass me! Not in front of her."

Sela stills.

Everyone and everything is quiet for a moment.

"Mom, listen to me," Darius starts. "Zalmon tried to kill Mah—"

Before Darius can get his sister's name out, Sela loses it. She runs manically around the room, holding her ear. She grabs a pillow from Mahlah's bed and holds it over Darius's mouth.

Darius is too strong for her and frees himself. "Get off me! What's the matter with you? I couldn't breathe! You trying to kill me?"

Sela winces as if in pain. She holds her head to the side, favoring the apparent sensitivity.

Abram is cozy at home, dressed casually, reading the Book in bed. His phone rings. He shoots a look of disgust at the device, annoyed by its intrusion. He tries to ignore it but eventually answers its incessant chirps.

"It's late," is Abram's hello.

An operator speaks into the other end. "Sir? There seems to be suspicious commotion with a Datura."

Abram rolls his eyes. "Follow the routine," he suggests. "Send a shock wave."

"I did, sir. No change," the operator says. She hesitates then adds, "It's Sela Anah, from your special interests list, sir."

Abram bolts up. He reaches over and turns a dial on a stereo receiver in his bedroom.

"Channel the Datura through to me, then disengage immediately. I'll handle her from here."

KILL

Thanks to the chip behind Sela's ear, the commotion at the Anah house is now broadcast through Abram's home stereo. But the chip doesn't just send signals — it also receives them. At the touch of Abram's fingertip, a button blasts a jolt of excruciating pain into Sela's neck. It reverberates from her head deep into her spine, causing her to collapse on Mahlah's bedroom floor.

"What the fuck is the matter with you?" Darius yells at his mother, certain she's mid-Datura episode, craving the attention of the room.

Priya has witnessed way more than she wanted to. She spots a clear pathway to the bedroom door and runs for it.

"Please don't go!" Darius yells. "My world is falling apart here. If you leave, I will have no contact with reality."

Abram's smile is menacing. He leans in for the broadcast. He believes that Darius is begging his Life Match Zuriel to comfort him.

Priya inches closer to an escape.

Sela stands back up again. This time, she assumes a different stature — one more resilient — but she closes her eyes, unsure what to do next.

"Wake up, Mom! Mahlah has a disease! They gave her a fake Death Date —" Darius is cut off as Sela lunges at him, wide-eyed with panic. She pleads with him, violently shaking her head.

"Yes!" Darius yells. "They gave her a fake Death Date so she would kill herself there!"

With both hands, Sela covers her son's big mouth again. They wrestle, banging into Mahlah's furniture and knocking framed photos to the floor.

"I need you to stop!" Darius manages to say.

"I know you do, but I can't!"

Darius doesn't know what she means.

Abram sends a jolt to Sela's neck. She bends in pain.

"What do you mean you can't?"

Sela leans in to whisper, "You're going to get yourself killed."

Abram sends two quick jolts in succession. He listens to the agonized cries of his Match. "Stop!" Sela's words splash out the speakers and ripple through Abram's bedroom. He smirks and sends another jolt, holding the button longer than before.

Darius tries to pry his mother's hand from the side of her head. She jumps.

"Please stop!" Sela begs.

"Stop what? Who are you talking to?" Darius shoots a look of embarrassment in Priya's direction.

"It's no bother," Priya lies. "I've seen Datura episodes before."
But Priya has never once experienced it to this degree.

"Darius," Sela says. "You're right. You're right about everything." She cries … partially in pain, partially in relief.

Darius steps back.

Priya waits in the doorway and watches this trainwreck.

Sela receives jolt after jolt but finds the strength to stand.

"They're listening," she yelps through the pain. Blood trickles between the fingers of the hand she holds against her skin.
"They're punishing me. They control us!"

"Control who? Daturas? You're bleeding!" Guilt pangs Darius's
insides.

Sela is doubled over by the rapid-fire pulses from her puppe-
teer, Abram.

"I'm so … so proud of you, Darius —"

And with that, she falls to the floor.

Darius rushes to her and tries to revive her.

Priya runs out of the bedroom, down the stairs, and out the
front door.

Abram leans over his technology. His hand shakes over the
row of controls he just manipulated. Well aware of what he's
done to Sela, his eyes glaze over, and he stares ahead. Then, he
snaps to, surges past his reflection in the mirror, grabs a sweater,
and storms off.

Back in Mahlah's room, Darius shakes his mother. She doesn't
respond.

He shakes her harder, then harder again.

Nothing.

Sela's heavy, lifeless head falls to the side, and blood spills
down her neck.

Darius's anger yields to desperation.

"Mom?" he tries.

Although used to the despondent nature of a Datura, nothing could have prepared Darius for this level of moroseness. In his despair and confusion, Darius doesn't know what to do other than wipe the bangs from his mother's eyes and push back her long locks away from the blood.

As he does so, Darius inadvertently feels the spot from which the blood trails. He rubs the strange bump. Is it a muscle knot? Is it akin to First Blood pimples? What is it?

He tries to move it. It budges a bit, but it seems to be rooted.

Darius buries his head in the side of his mother's neck. A sadness unlike anything he's ever experienced, even worse than when his dad Left, overcomes him. He heaves, bawling, willing his dead mother's eyes to open.

Noise from outside steals Darius's attention — a car pulling up in front of the house and shutting off its engine. Then, the sound of two car doors being closed, but gently, as if in an attempt to be silent.

Something about the sound, or lack of it, rubs Darius the wrong way. He stares at his dead mother — longing for her guidance now, more than ever before. Her breathless, motionless being lay heavy in his arms.

Darius hears his front door ease open. His heart pounds so loudly he can barely make sense of his thoughts. He looks at his little sister sleeping soundly on the floor. He moves out from under his mother and rushes to his little sister to hoist her over his shoulder.

Footsteps try to ascend the Anah house staircase quietly, but Darius is on to them. He drops Mahlah as gingerly as he can into her closet, tucks her feet in, and shuts the door. His focus returns to his mother.

Darius hears the familiar creaks in all of the memorized spots of his upper hallway floor. Whoever is in his house is about to find him.

Darius places a desk chair against the doorknob, hoping it will buy him enough time. Before he runs to Mahlah's window, he scoops up his lifeless mother with a strength that renders her light as a baby girl. He cradles Sela's head against his chest and her legs hang over his arm. The bedroom door is pushed against the chair from the outside of it. The men don't say a word, but they abandon silence as they work to break down the door. Wood splinters with their brute blows. Just as they clear a hole through the wood, Darius struggles to hang on to his mother and climb out Mahlah's window. He escapes onto the rooftop landing, then down into his pitch-black backyard, somehow unscathed physically but annihilated emotionally.

The men look out the window, dumbfounded as to what to do next. When they return to their car, one of them asks the man in the shadows of the back seat, "Should we hunt him down, sir?"

Abram doesn't even entertain their stupidity with a response. Rather, he digresses.

"When my father entrusted me with this position, I told him that video surveillance was necessary and that times had changed. 'We need to watch,' I said over and over and over. His order was to keep Zalmon running the way it was."

"I can drive down these side streets, sir," the beefed-up man in the front pipes up.

"We need to be sure of who else was in that room tonight."

PROCESS

Sela's blood covers Darius. He glances down at her and it steals his breath away. He shakes his head and continues to run … almost in circles.

Noah happens to be driving by, or so he hopes it appears. He doesn't want Darius to think he's stalking him, but Noah senses dread in the teenager and feels inclined to check in on him.

"Kid!" Noah yells before Darius dips out of sight.

Noah doesn't give up. He's been in this world long enough to know when he needs to step up and step in. He turns down a side road and flickers his headlights on Darius's back.

Darius turns to look. He can't even form words. He's in shock. Stuck between Noah's car and a dead end, he falls to his knees and drops Sela, succumbing to a flood of tears before Noah helps them into the car.

There's a time to pry and a time not to. Despite not being afforded a Life Match nor children of his own in Zalmon on account of his skin color, Noah's instinct is that Darius needs a quiet kind of support now — a comfortable silence that offers him both space and the platform to speak, should he feel ready. He tries not to stare at the corpse in his backseat through his rearview mirror. He's only ever read about them in the forbidden books.

Darius doesn't know how to stop his tears. They just keep coming.

Noah speeds through Zalmon. He reaches the familiar spot in the trees and busts through.

Darius's tears have yielded to panicked paces over the small floor in this moody room with Aysa where Sela is on the floor covered by a white sheet.

"Blood? A chip?" Aysa tries for clarity.

Darius can't even respond.

"Darius, I've heard a lot of things, but …"

Darius wishes someone could take this pain away from him. He replays Mahlah's attack over and over then switches to whatever went wrong with his mother. Every time he blinks, he relives Sela's final moments of agony.

But Aysa is the one shaking his head incessantly now. "I've just never heard anyone describe a … Natural Death?"

Darius lifts his clenched fist high in the air and rushes Aysa. He strikes him across his face. "What's natural about all that?" he screams as he tries to swing at Aysa again, but Aysa catches his fist mid-air. This doesn't stop Darius from whipping Aysa to the ground.

"Control yourself, Darius." Aysa maintains as much composure as he can.

Darius mounts Aysa in a wrestling hold and renders Aysa helpless, but just as he's about to pummel him, he stops at the dignified look in the man's eyes as he surrenders. No one deserves this wrath, beyond whoever is responsible for his mother's death. Darius feels like he doesn't know much right now, but he at least knows it has nothing to do with this man who helped save his sister.

Darius jumps off Aysa, pants, then turns and runs out.

Abram sits in a dark red room filled with more computers, stereo systems, and receivers. The disgust on his face is nearly as loud as the beeps and hums of the equipment. Two henchmen are still with him.

Abram presses a button to replay muffled audio from the night before:

"You do it, Darius! I can't!" Priya's cries echo through the room.

Abram stops the audio.

"There. Who was that? Both she and Darius saw Sela die." Abram fidgets with two Datura chips in his hands. "We must silence the naysayers who would corrupt our civil peace and tranquility."

The two men nod in agreement.

"Is it the voice of his Life Match, sir?" one of them asks.

"Zuriel Levi? Yes. Probably," Abram concedes.

"What about the little sister?" the other man asks.

"I infer that she passed out. Given my knowledge of her illness and what they probably injected, she didn't see a thing. It explains how he stuffed her in a closet." A cynical laugh escapes Abram.

He stops.

"We must find them."

TRY

Priya and her mother, Priscilla, browse the grocery store together. Aside from a small height difference and more laugh lines, Priscilla is the spitting image of her daughter.

The grocery store is pristine. Rows upon rows of healthy foods boast vibrant colors and succulent juiciness. The fruits and vegetables stack high and mighty. There is no trace of forbidden food in this establishment.

As soon as Priscilla passes a post, a screen displays and reads out her family's grocery list, then suggests some favorites that Priscilla may have overlooked. Priscilla listens while noting if each thing is in her grocery cart. Indeed, she has missed a few.

As she walks away from the post, Priscilla's ad flips back to a generic one.

Thank you for shopping at Zalmon's Best grocery store.

"Zalmon's only," Priya mutters.

"What was that?" Priscilla asks.

"It's no matter." Priya keeps her thoughts to herself while the commercial continues.

Your body's fuel station, where natural and locally grown foods are sold at reasonable prices and trades.

The ad plays visuals of children playing, running, kicking soccer balls, throwing footballs, flinging frisbees, and skipping rope.

At Zalmon's Best, we know your body is your temple.

It cuts to families paying at the register, smiling, and leaving. A bright, bubbly logo featuring *Zalmon's Best* flashes across the screen.

Priya holds a small basket in her arms, mostly to stop herself from fidgeting nervously. She hasn't been able to calm her nerves since last night. Every sound makes her jump, every young girl pulls her thoughts back to Mahlah's convulsions, and anything red is Sela's blood. As Priya passes the post, it tunes back into her family's broadcasted specials and grocery list. But to her surprise, the list wipes clean and is replaced by one for the Anah family. Priya panics; did she will that to happen? Is someone reading her mind? Is Darius in the store? Is Mahlah? Are they behind her? She freaks out and drops her basket.

By the time she grabs it and stands up, the list is back to hers. She attributes what she saw to a hallucination.

"We'll just grab a few more things." Priscilla's voice calms Priya.

A few more things ... Yeah, Priya can handle that. "I'll help," she offers.

In the healthy carbs aisle, Priya studies the images on the boxes of her three choices: rice, pasta, or maybe some breadcrumbs to spice up the fish. She opts for the breadcrumbs, remembering how her dad used to dip fresh fish into an egg mixture then whirl it around in a bowlful of crumbs before tossing it onto a baking sheet. She starts to head back toward her mother and goes to toss the breadcrumbs into her basket.

Darius suddenly jumps into view, and she drops the box. It splits open, and the crumbs spill. They bounce all over the floor like off-white bracelet beads.

Priya and Darius both bend down to clean up.

Priya whispers, "I don't think I ever want to see you again, Darius."

Ignoring her declaration, Darius curbs his intensity into a whisper as well. "They're after me."

"Then I definitely don't ever want to see you again." Priya goes to stand up, but Darius pulls her back down.

"I'm sorry," he says, upset that she flinched at his touch. "Did I hurt you?"

"It's not that you hurt me," Priya starts. "It's that I don't know what is happening! Please go," she says.

"Priya, please." Instinctively, Darius reaches for her hand.

"I'll scream!"

Darius's eyes water.

Priya softens ever so slightly. "Look, I know you're sad about your mom. I just ... I'm so scared, Darius."

"I'm scared too," Darius admits. "I saw something — something behind my mother's ear ... covered in blood."

"I told you it was horrible — a Natural Death. You didn't believe me." She starts to stand up again, but Darius yanks her back down.

Priya screams. Darius tries to cover her mouth. She struggles and screams some more. Darius lets her go and runs as fast as he can out of the store.

PINPOINT

Zuriel hums as she trots around the sanitized room, cleaning up. She wears protective gear as outlined in the safety protocols for assisting Welcome Releases. The gear is white, thick, and bulky.

Abram spies on Zuriel through one-way mirrored glass. He studies her movements. He admires how meticulous she is and how she's doing everything by the book. She places equipment back where it belongs, readies restraints for the next time, and takes off her gear and hangs it all in the proper bin. When she's finished, she fixes her hair while looking in the mirror — unaware that she is staring right at Abram on the other side.

Abram heads out into the hall then joins Zuriel in the Welcome Release room.

"Mr. Job?" Zuriel is surprised to see Abram at Quiet End.

"Miss Levi." Abram walks around like he owns the place. Zuriel doesn't know it's because he does.

"Final visit with someone?" Zuriel asks. "Can I help you find the right room?" She is professional.

Abram shakes his head as he listens carefully to the inflections of her voice. Then he says, "A good leader just knows when it's time to get involved."

"Leader?" Zuriel is confused.

Meanwhile, Priya rushes into the front lobby of Quiet End. She nods the quickest and least engaged hello to the receptionist. She looks up at the clock and realizes that she's later than she thought. She hustles down the hallway.

"I … I'm sorry Mr. Job. I don't know what you're getting at," says Zuriel.

Abram leans into her space. "Where were you last night?" he asks.

"Home," she answers.

"At home?" Abram questions.

"Yes."

"Alone?"

She thinks about it. "My parents were out … Yes."

"How convenient," Abram snarks.

"Sorry?" Zuriel isn't sure she heard him right.

Out in the long hallway, Priya takes off her coat and straightens her pink Quiet End uniform over her thighs. She glances at her posted to-do list before she notices that the door at the end of the hallway — the Welcome Release room door — is ajar slightly, which is odd. She heads to it with the intention of closing it but realizes that there are people chatting in there. She lifts her fist to knock and announce her presence but stops herself at the sound of Abram's voice.

"I know you were with Darius Anah last night, and I know what you saw."

Priya's jaw drops.

"I don't know what you're talking about," Zuriel says.

Abram bursts out laughing. "I heard you, Zuriel!"

Priya starts to shake.

"Heard me what?" Zuriel asks. "I wasn't with Darius. I haven't seen him in a couple of days." Her calm is almost eerie.

Abram stares deeply into her eyes and shakes his head.

Zuriel shrugs. "If you don't believe me, ask Sela."

Abram slams his fist down on a countertop.

"As his Life Match, you are obligated to do what's best for him. So I wouldn't harbor ill feelings if you were there," Abram lies.

"Mr. Job, I understand that."

Trying to get a rise out of her, Abram takes one last shot. "I hate to tell you this Zuriel, but I believe he's going Datura."

"Darius is?" Zuriel is confused.

Abram heads toward the door. "Send him to me at once," he orders.

Knowing he'll spot her if she doesn't act quickly, Priya runs down the hallway as fast as she can.

In Abram's haste, he's not far behind her.

Priya makes it back out to the receptionist area. She's out of breath.

"Everything okay?" the receptionist asks her.

Priya nods. She sees Abram coming in her direction. With nowhere to hide, she buries her face in a file folder.

Abram makes it to the foyer area. He spots Priya right away. "Miss?" he says.

Priya looks up from the folder. "Mm-hmm?" she musters with as little of her voice as possible.

"Is that today's Welcome Release schedule?" It's a question he full well knows the answer to.

Priya nods. She wonders if her trembling is as noticeable to Abram and the receptionist as it is to her.

"May I?" Abram reaches for the folder.

Priya hesitates then shakes her head very slowly. She mumbles, "It's confidential."

Abram laughs and taps her on the arm. She jumps.

"Well-trained." Abram is pleased. He begins to leave.

Priya hyperventilates as she bolts in the opposite direction.

"Oh, miss," Abram says, turning to her once more.

Priya stops dead and looks at him.

"I believe it's that way." Abram points to the hall where Priya works.

She manages a thumbs-up sign and turns to go that way.

Zuriel zooms past both of them and whips out the Quiet End front doors.

Priya hides behind a corner and looks down at her phone calling list. Of course, Darius isn't on there. She wishes he were, more than ever.

BURY

It's far after curfew, but Darius doesn't care. He sits in the back seat of Noah's car, ducked all the way down and out of people's sight. Noah sits in the front seat, pretending to read his Zalmon newspaper.

Darius is on the phone with Mahlah, who is all alone at home, oblivious to everything that happened but irate.

"Darius? Where are you? And where is Mom?"

Darius swallows hard. "I don't know. She's Datura. She could be anywhere."

"She's never done this before."

"Don't worry about her. Worry about yourself." Darius can't bring himself to tell Mahlah the truth. How could he without devastating her? But what should he tell her instead? That their mother Left? That would be equally as traumatic to a young girl who believes in Zalmon, and just another lie on top of lies.

Instead of telling her, Darius changes the subject.

"Are you okay with those needles?"

Mahlah refuses to answer.

"Are you okay?" Darius repeats. "With those needles?"

Mahlah hangs up.

Just as she does, there is a knock at her front door.

Mahlah makes her way downstairs and looks through the peephole. To her shock, it's Priya. Mahlah unlocks the door to let her in.

Priya is out of breath.

"Darius isn't here," Mahlah tells her.

"Where is he?"

"I don't know."

"Are you okay?" Priya softens, thinking that not only is this poor kid in recovery, she just lost her mother and must be in agony.

"Are *you* okay?" Mahlah mirrors the sentiment, although for different reasons. She's never seen Priya look this distraught, and Mahlah fears it's her fault on account of last night's episode, which she vaguely recollects the beginning of.

Priya wipes tears from her eyes.

"My brother has a real habit of making girls cry."

"It's not that. It's just … you've been through so, so much this past while, and me? You ask about me? You're the sweetest, honestly."

Mahlah shrugs. She feels much better, whatever it was. Or is. She wonders why Priya is making such a fuss over her.

"Do you mind if I come in and stay here?" Priya asks. "I really don't think you should be by yourself."

"Don't worry. They'll come home soon," Mahlah says. She's nervous about the socialization rules. There's no valid reason for Priya to be in their home.

Priya notes the *they'll*. She gasps. Mahlah doesn't know about her mother.

Priya won't budge. Mahlah, tired of the standoff, lets her in.

Aysa, Noah, and Darius stare at Sela's corpse in the middle of the room — each is having a different reaction.

Noah wonders how the people who loved her are doing, if she died filled with happiness or if living as a Datura voided the good memories from her existence. He can relate to her diseased years, in a sense. He is more robotic than the average man on account of having little to live for. What is a man if not a loved one, or a provider, or a leader? Noah has never known anything different; he was born with rare skin twenty shades darker than most, and as a curious and observant citizen of Zalmon, he knows he got the raw end of the deal. Even in the Underground ... Sure he's been linked to women romantically, but just in an experimental way — like he's a notch on their belts. Aboveground, he's not permitted to fall in love, and underground, he's not taken seriously.

Aysa looks at Sela's cadaver as an opportunity. Back when he was a contributing member in Medical Training, they had dummies to work on, of course, but the rubber mannequins didn't do things justice. Here, Aysa can see how cold Sela is. How her fingertips have blued. How her cheeks have grayed. There is nothing sentimental about it to him. Medicine is Aysa's calling. Aboveground, he did it and did it well, but the life was getting to him. He knew he was being overlooked during promotion periods. He was always on Annual Check duty and was never able to reach his full potential — never called up to the big leagues. Anonymous notes in his locker warned him that he asked "too many questions." But how does a person learn if they don't ask questions? It took years to convince his Life Match to escape to the Underground, but he managed. Now she seeks the company of others more than she ever did him, and it doesn't bother him in the least. Aysa isn't sure why — there's no medical reasoning and no mention of it in the Book — but he's always felt a pull to his same sex. He is attracted to some of the men in his life on a level he can't, and never will, articulate, so the facade with his Life Match works. They're together but not.

For some reason, when Darius looks at Sela now, he's taken back to his childhood. Why, after the death of a loved one, do we recall the good times over the bad? For the past five years, Sela has been completely Datura as if following a strict manual. But prior to that, his mother was warm, loving, nurturing, energetic, and fun. She had a lust for life that was contagious. While her two children were toddlers, she would scoop them up and cuddle them for as long as they could stand it. And the love she extended to her Life Match? Undeniable passion, faithfulness, and loyalty. There was nothing Darius's father could do to upset her. She had unparalleled patience and bottomless forgiveness. Darius wants nothing more right now than to tell his mother how she made him feel during the early years of his life, and that he will carry those days with him. Above all else, he wants to tell her he's sorry for being such a shitty son, for not being the kind of person she raised him to be, for questioning her at every turn, and for misunderstanding her intentions.

He should have known.

"I don't have the equipment to burn her," Aysa says.

"Burn her?" Darius is disgusted.

"I think that's what's done with dead bodies."

"Have respect, Aysa," Noah says, moving between them. "Darius, from what we've read, it's customary for a human to be cremated — it means their solid state is transformed into vapor and ashes. Their energy is released into our world. That way, they're never really gone. Isn't that right, Aysa?"

"Just like I said. Burn her."

After some thought, Darius asks, "But you don't have the right equipment?"

"It's not hygienic to do it in our pits, otherwise I would," Aysa says.

"We could bury her," Noah suggests.

Darius and Aysa turn to him like he's insane.

"Absolutely not," says Darius.

"Hear me out. The idea behind cremation is to have her essence released into air molecules. But if we bury her under the Underground, then …"

Aysa gets into it now. "Then her" — he side-eyes Noah — "essence will filter through the clay and soil, leading all the way to the real trees. And I suppose parts of her will always be in the leaves."

"And beyond." Noah smiles.

Darius thinks about it for a long while. "Let's bury her," he decides.

CONFRONT

Darius sits alone beside a hollow, waxy tree behind his school. A rustle of fake grass catches his attention.

It's Zuriel.

"School's over, Darius," she says. "You'll be late for —"

"I know."

"What are you doing out here?"

"My mother's dead," Darius blurts, his tears heisted by anger.

Zuriel shakes her head slowly. She presumes he's being figurative and doesn't know what to say.

"Right in front of me," Darius continues. "No Card. No warning. Bam! Dead. What have I done?"

He's losing it, she thinks. She tries to tap him on the back, but Darius swats her hand away.

"You should talk to Abram," Zuriel suggests.

"Abram?!"

Zuriel averts her eyes. "He is so close with your mother. You can trust him. It seems like you're in need of good counseling — time with someone who knows the Book really well."

"No one knows the Book better than you, Zuriel."

"I wish that were true, but …"

"I can't trust anyone."

"Look at me," Zuriel starts. "Go to Abram. I saw him. He wants to help you."

Abram opens his front door to find Darius, drenched from the rain. A lightning bolt smites the air as Darius enters. Thunder rumbles.

Abram fakes a warm smile before he closes and double-locks the front door. Darius has never seen locks on a house's door before. They're not needed in Zalmon.

"Let me get you a towel, Darius," Abram says.

Abram heads upstairs, and Darius turns to snoop around the living room. It's his first time in the man's house.

Darius notes the pictures of Abram on the walls of his living room. He assumes the other people in them are friends and family whom he's surprised he's never met, given the Second Match link.

The living room is connected to a grand office through a tiny hallway. Darius makes his way to an enormous hardwood desk. He glides his finger along a heavy silver letter opener with a sharp tip. He flips through a stack of papers, noting nothing in particular.

Just as he hears Abram start to make his way down the stairs, Darius eyes two small metal chips with long prongs on the edges.

The ends of the chips resemble the shape that Darius is sure he felt behind his mother's ear.

Darius whips around just as Abram finds him in the office.

Abram wraps a towel over Darius's shoulders. Darius jumps.

"Have a seat." Abram steers him toward a chair.

Darius leans against Abram's desk instead. "Nah, I'm good," he maintains.

"Have a seat."

Darius takes a very deep breath then sits down slowly.

Abram stands tall in front of him and stares into his eyes. "Let's play a little game," he teases. "Some tit for tat, if you will."

Darius cowers from Abram's intense gaze.

"I'll tell you a little something, then you'll tell me a little something. Sound fun?" Abram's question is rhetorical, and they both know it.

Still, Darius shakes his head.

"Good boy," Abram says, ignoring the gesture. "I'm it," he chuckles. After a very long pause, he declares, "I'm the most powerful man in Zalmon."

Darius raises an eyebrow.

"I'm the … Leader, if you will." Darius hides his shock. Abram points to him calmly. "Your turn."

"I … I did not know that," Darius says.

Abram smirks. Darius doesn't budge. So Abram continues, "And I know where you've been running off to, little rat."

Darius sweats.

Abram smears a droplet with his finger. "It's okay, son." He laughs. "Let them all rot." He waits for Darius to say something. "You'll have to do much better than that, Darius." He circles Darius's chair with menacing steps. "Your mother …"

Darius straightens.

"She had a little secret, you see. And when people have secrets, we … well, let's just say we make sure they don't tell."

Darius can't swallow. He puts two and two together.

Abram points to Darius again.

There's a long silence.

Darius decides to play along.

"My mother," he starts. "She was killed."

Abram erupts in laughter. "Well played, son. Well played. That tat was a little more than I expected out of you."

Darius points to Abram. "Your go."

Abram's demeanor darkens. "Someone else saw your mother die that night, and it wasn't Zuriel Levi."

"No. It wasn't." Darius tenses.

Abram waits for him to continue, but Darius points at Abram again.

"Who was there with you?" Abram asks.

"You want me to play out of turn?"

Abram's nose flares. Darius locks eyes with him. "You tried to kill my sister."

Abram chokes on his own spit. Then he shakes his head and tuts. "I underestimated your skill in this little game, Darius. But you're wrong. If all had gone according to plan, Mahlah would have had herself happily terminated, of course."

"How convenient."

Abram smiles. "We do very little unsolicited killing. Only under dire circumstances." He pats Darius on the head.

"I think I'm it, right?"

Abram smirks. "I believe so, yes."

"You wanted me here to … silence me." He motions to the

chips on Abram's desk. "With one of those."

"It's a temporary one, but yes, Darius. That's why I wanted you to come." Abram's smile fades. "You know, for such a smart young man, you're missing a strategic opportunity here."

"There's nothing to gain from you."

Abram leans right into Darius face, only inches away. "Aren't you the least bit curious why your mother was silenced?"

Until this moment, no, he wasn't. His stomach aches instantly.

"Ask me. Ask me who, Darius. Whom did your mother see die?"

Darius freezes.

"I believe you were … twelve when it happened."

Darius starts to shake.

"He was in your driveway, just out of your sight, but your mother was with him. He was about to go to work, if I recall correctly. And his heart — his useless, weak heart — just … stopped." Abram laughs.

Tears spill from Darius's eyes.

"No one's ever Left Zalmon, you fool. We just … you know … we have a Natural Death folklore to uphold." Abram walks over to get one of the metal chips. "Your poor little sister — still looking for your dead mother. She'll tell me who else was in the room with you that night." Abram yanks Darius's head to the side. He holds the prongs of the chip close to his neck under ear. "I greatly look forward to listening in on your long, disadvantaged life, Datura." He pulls out a scalpel and goes to slice through Darius's skin.

Darius whips the silver letter opener out from under his shirt —

And thrusts it into Abram's side.

Abram screams. He grabs Darius by the neck.

Darius twists the opener.

Abram lets go.

Darius runs.

CONVINCE

Darius scurries between the cars in the parking lot. He cannot find Noah anywhere. Panic consumes him, and he feels a tightness in his chest. Desperate times call for desperate measures. Darius rushes at a random car and yells at its driver.

"Get out!"

"No way," the driver says.

Darius smashes his foot against the door handle over and over until the handle snaps off and the door opens.

Darius grabs the driver by the throat and drags him out of the car. A few of the other drivers look on in disbelief, but no one wants to be a hero.

Darius throws the driver to the ground and rips the keys from his pocket.

He jumps into the car and fumbles to start it. He's never driven a car — he's only watched Drivers start an engine. As he stalls it a few times, some of the other drivers come out of the woodwork to throw futile words at the teenager.

The engine turns, and Darius takes off on a crash course through Zalmon. He knocks down picket fences, rips up turf, and bangs into medians.

Until he arrives at his house.

He parks diagonally in his driveway, gets out, and whips up his walkway. He startles Priya, who is on his couch.

Mahlah is up in her room.

"We gotta go!" Darius yells at the top of his lungs. His adrenaline leaves no room for normalcy. He wants to tell them everything, but not here, not like this.

Priya huddles into herself and pulls a blanket up to her chin.

"Now!" Darius is angry that no one seems to be listening or taking him seriously.

Mahlah flies down the stairs.

"Go grab yourself some clothes," Darius orders. "Meet me in the car."

Mahlah has never seen her brother so dead serious. She does as she's told.

Priya, on the other hand, doesn't move.

"I'm not messing around, Priya. They're on to me. They'll be on to you!"

"Me? Why me?" Priya gasps.

Darius lowers his voice, afraid Mahlah will hear. "Because you saw my mother die, and you and I both know that wasn't a Natural Death. Stop being so naive, please! I can take us someplace safe."

"I'm not naive, and I'm not going!"

Darius can see equal parts ferocity and fear in Priya's eyes. He tries to calm himself. "I want you …," he says. "I want you with me."

"I'm only here because I wanted to know that you're okay," says Priya. "I know it now. Well, *okay* is an overstatement, but … I'm leaving now."

"They'll kill you."

Mahlah is downstairs now, behind him. Darius grabs her arm — she jumps. Darius leads them outside but turns once more to Priya.

Who just shakes her head.

Darius and Mahlah run to the stolen car in the driveway and peel away at breakneck speed.

Back home, Priya tosses and turns in her own bed. She cannot stop the thoughts from running rampant in her mind. She's normally a great sleeper who easily surrenders to slumber, but these days? No way.

There is a knock on her bedroom door. Priya freezes.

"Can I come in?" It's her mother, Priscilla.

She doesn't answer.

"Priya? There are two men outside who need to see you about a matter."

Priya shoots upright. She isn't sure what to do or say. "Tell them I'm out, Mom."

"They would never believe that." She laughs. "It's well past curfew."

"Well, just tell them anyway!" Priya shouts.

"What's wrong? Who are they?"

"Tell them!" Priya insists. "If it's so important, they'll leave me a message."

Priya waits for her mother to make her way back down the stairs before she bolts to her bedroom window and peeks out to watch the two men retreat to their car and pull away.

Priscilla is back outside Priya's room. "There was no message," she says. "Can I come in?"

Priya opens the door.

"They just needed to ask you some questions."

Priya tries to shrug it off, but Priscilla notes the trembling of her daughter's hands.

"What pressed you to lie to them? Tell me what's going on."

"It's not important."

"They sure looked important, Priya."

Priya sits back down on her bed, and the tears start flowing.

Priscilla walks over to her and taps her on the arm. "It's about that boy, isn't it? The one from the grocery store."

Priya shrugs.

Priscilla gets the hint. "I'm here for you, Priya." She turns to go but pauses to say, "For advice you won't find in the Book."

As soon as her mother closes the door behind her, Priya whips on warmer clothes and escapes out her window.

HIDE

As Darius leads Mahlah through the Underground corridors, she stops at an open door. Inside the room, a group of people in their early twenties are listening to loud, heavy-bass music. A few people smile at her. One, the woman with the thin, tattooed arms, waves.

A couple makes out in the corner. Mahlah gawks at their intertwined tongues and forbidden, frisky hands. It takes her breath away.

Darius yanks Mahlah away from the door.

A teenaged boy with flaming-red hair, freckles, and piercing green eyes approaches Mahlah. He's wearing a black T-shirt, black jeans, and black sneakers, all highlighting his uniqueness.

"Hi, I'm Matias," he says, reaching out his hand to shake Mahlah's. It's a gesture she's never seen before — she doesn't know what he wants her to do with his hand. She doesn't want to double-tap it because this guy is a stranger.

Darius comes over and swats the guy's hand down. "Knock it off," he warns. "She's only thirteen."

Matias mumbles an apology, all the while smiling at Mahlah, who blushes.

Darius leads her further down the hallway. "You shouldn't have seen all that. You're way too young."

"Shouldn't have seen *that*? I shouldn't be down here, period." Mahlah says. "Mom's going to kill you when she finds out."

Darius sees Aysa is within earshot — he shoots him a look not to intervene. Aysa complies against his better judgment and heads into a room.

"We have to talk," Darius says to Mahlah. "About Mom."

"How did you find this place?" Mahlah is too consumed by curiosity to be hooked by Darius's bait.

"Don't worry about that right now."

"You've made a real mess, Darius."

"I'll fix it," Darius promises.

Mahlah rolls her eyes.

Aysa comes back out and runs up to Darius. He grabs him and pulls him all the way to his office.

"Matias," Aysa calls out over his shoulder, "watch the girl."

"Absolutely not!" Darius shouts.

"Just keep her occupied," Aysa tells Matias. "I need a minute with this one. Now!"

Matias leads Mahlah into the treats room as Aysa throws Darius into the office, slams the door shut behind them, and locks it.

"What's the matter with you?" Darius asks.

"You've got a lot of nerve coming back here after what I just saw."

"What? Why? Why wouldn't I?"

Aysa switches on the large screen in his office. He flips through channels then stops on one before he leans in to turn up the volume. The public service announcement has already started, and it shows Abram sitting in the doctor's office with his hand over a blood-soaked bandage on his side. Abram is mid-spiel. "... His name is Darius Anah. He's just under six feet tall. He has brown, buzz-cut hair and very blue eyes." Abram removes the bandage, exposes the gash from the letter opener, and winces in pain. "He's armed and very dangerous."

A photo of Darius flashes on the screen before a Datura newscaster takes over. "Most Daturas are nonviolent, but sometimes, I'm afraid to say, sometimes we pass a point of no return." Security footage (footage that will no doubt be a surprise to all Zalmons) shows Darius running through the parking lot, forcing that driver from his vehicle, and assaulting him. The newscaster continues, "Darius's motives are unclear. He speaks nonsense, and we fear that he will stop at nothing to ruin everything ... to ruin Zalmon. Together, we cannot let that happen. If you spot him, keep your distance and report him to authorities at once." The newscaster glances at Abram, who nods approval at the messaging.

Finally, a montage of happy, healthy families graces the screen. "In Zalmon, we unite." The photo of Darius reappears. "If you capture Darius Anah, you will be rewarded threefold: a Finance-Free Card, a Vocation Break Card, and a Quiet End Retirement Package."

Aysa mutes the rest of the announcement. He fixes his stare on Darius, while Darius stares at his own image up on the massive screen.

"Hand it over," Aysa orders.

"I don't have a weapon. It was his own letter opener."

"Savage," Aysa declares.

"Are you going to turn me in?"

"I have half a mind to."

Darius puts both of his hands out in front of him as if Aysa is ready to tie him up and drag him in.

Aysa clubs him on the side of the head.

"You're anti-Zalmon!" Darius yells at Aysa. "You disagree with everything! Why do you care what he says? What is the point of this place, anyway?"

"It's about people who stay. People who stay and manage to live freely. Outsiders fuel our rebellion."

Darius laughs at the word.

Aysa ignores him. "We're people who stand tall and don't Leave."

"Listen to me, Aysa." Darius is more serious than he's ever been. "No one's ever really Left."

Aysa clubs him on the side of the head again. "What is wrong with you? Make sense, Datura."

Darius leans right up to his face, ignoring the insult. "Dead! They're all dead."

Aysa slams Darius into a chair. "Dead? Dead from Leaving? What's out there?"

"Nobody knows what's out there because nobody's Left!"

Aysa goes to smack Darius again, but Darius catches his hand.

"Are you listening to me, Aysa? No. One. Has. Ever. Left. Zalmon. All those people who we thought Left? They all died ... unexpectedly. They were deaths Zalmon couldn't predict because Zalmon doesn't know! It only knows what's self-serving. And anyone who witnessed those deaths suffers tracking and warning shots of pain for the rest of their lives to keep them silent!"

"Datura." Aysa gets it.

"What?" Mahlah's small voice comes through the locked door. Doom devours Darius.

"Go away, Mahlah!" Darius calls. "You should be with Freckles."

"Open the door!" Mahlah yells.

Aysa nods to Darius.

As soon as it's unlocked —

"Dad is dead?" Mahlah's eyes well with tears.

Darius is at a loss for words.

"Yes, Mahlah." Aysa steps up. "Your father is dead."

"Who are you? Stop talking to me. Is Dad dead, Darius?"

Darius nods.

Mahlah falls slowly to the ground. "And that's why Mom is Datura?"

"Your mother is dead too, Mahlah," says Aysa.

Darius is enraged. "What is the matter with you, man?!"

Darius and Mahlah stand close at Sela's burial site, near the edge of the hidden entrance to the Underground. Darius puts his arm around his little sister. At first, the contact catches her off guard, but then she leans into it. She cries.

"She saved your life," Darius says.

"When?" Mahlah asks.

"The night you were all torn up from your illness. She blasted into the room and stuck some insulin in your belly when Priya and I were too scared to do it."

The silence is thick. It lasts longer than either of them can stand, but they don't know what to say.

"I think we're alone now," Mahlah says. "No Gramps. No Grams. No father. No mother. What do they do with kids like us?"

"I'm almost an adult, Mahlah. I will take care of you."

"I heard the PSA, Darius. We're in big trouble, aren't we?"

"You're not. But I might be."

FIGHT

Noah has been on high alert all day. He continues to stand guard while Darius meanders about the Underground. Noah hasn't eaten, he hasn't slept, he hasn't even gone to the washroom for hours.

Four wide-eyed, focused, muscled men trample through the clay hallway, looking for someone.

Noah stands between them and Aysa's office.

"Out of our way, Nedab," one of the men says. "We don't want to have to mess you up like we did all the time in high school."

The men cackle.

One of them calls out, "I think I saw him! He just went that way!"

Mahlah comes out of Aysa's office to see what the commotion is about.

Noah plays dumb. "Who? Who went what way?"

"That kid! Anah!"

Noah stands firm. "He's harmless. Leave him be."

"I see, Nedab. You're hoarding him for yourself. You gonna turn him in? What're you gonna do with a Vocation Break Card?" The men laugh. "Play with yourself day and night?"

"Do they even let people that look like you into Quiet End?" They laugh some more.

Aysa comes out of his office then closes the door behind him. "Back up!" he shouts.

The men shuffle a bit, used to obeying orders.

"He's in my office," Aysa says, walking up to the group.

One of the men moves to the front. "Let me at him."

Not on Aysa's watch. "You will leave him alone."

"No, we won't."

Aysa tries to calm them. "The kid has insight."

"The kid's my ticket."

Mahlah interjects. "No."

The men turn to face the thirteen-year-old girl in the cold, dark Underground tunnel.

"Go home, kid," says one of the men. "This ain't no place for a young girl."

"Darius is my brother." She's scared, but she's proud.

Aysa thinks she's suicidal. He closes his eyes.

"Oh, is that so?" the guy mocks. "Your brother done some bad things, darlin." He grabs Mahlah and holds her by the neck.

Aysa starts toward them to protect her, but the other three men toss him against the wall. He falls to the floor.

"Hey, big brother!" the choker taunts loudly. "You may want to come get your sister while she's still got some air left."

Mahlah's face turns purple. She claws at the man's hands.

Darius rushes out of a different room, racing to help his sister. The man releases his choke hold on Mahlah. She crashes to the ground and fights to catch her breath.

The group of men restrain Darius and haul him aboveground.

DETAIN

At Quiet End, Priya is outside the employee entrance at the back. She looks around to make sure that no one else is in the vicinity then swipes her Vocation card.

The indicator light stays red. She swipes again. It refuses to turn green. Priya knows what this means: her access has been revoked. She hangs her head in her hands.

But then she hears footsteps from inside — someone is coming out. She hides behind the door as it swings outward and an employee exits. As they walk away, Priya moves stealthily and grabs the door before it shuts. She waits until the employee is out of sight then slips into the building unnoticed.

Inside, Priya sneaks into an office and grabs a folder from a desk. She opens it and scans the list of the day's Welcome Releases. She is intent on finding the people on the list, but just as she's about to leave the office, Zuriel enters.

"Priya? You're not on tonight."

"Nope. Just checking my Vocation Allowance for this week." Priya tucks the Welcome Releases folder behind her body.

"It's the same as any other, no?"

"I couldn't remember exactly. I want to open my Housing Funds nice and early like my parents did. They paid theirs off speedy-quick." *Speedy-quick* is a phrase Priya has never used in her life, but on account of nervousness, it escapes her.

"Lot of good that did your father," Zuriel chuckles. "He Left."

Priya ignores the jab.

"Seen Darius lately?" Zuriel asks.

Priya shakes her head and shrugs her shoulders. "No. He's your Life Match."

Zuriel glares into Priya's blue eyes. "For your own good, I suggest you go. You're forcing me to make a phone call."

Zuriel motions toward the phone as Priya runs out of the office.

Instead of running out of the building as Zuriel would suspect, Priya sneaks into the never-used Welcome Release Viewing Room. It is behind a one-way mirror, so she won't be spotted.

A car pulls up in front of Priya's house. It just … waits.

Priscilla glances out the front window at the sound of the idling vehicle. She takes a very deep breath, wondering what's in store for her.

Abram sits in his office and watches as the burly men who stole Darius from the Underground throw him across the room.

Darius is bruised and battered, and he curls up on the floor.

Abram gets up from his chair, walks over, and spits on Darius. The others laugh. Abram shuts them up with a flick of his hand.

Abram kneels to get right in Darius's face. "In the name of Zalmon, shame on you!"

The men scatter to the other side of the room to distance themselves from their furious leader.

"You will not deface all that I have worked so hard to provide!" Abram froths at the mouth.

"What, exactly, you son of a bitch?" Darius speaks up.

The men return to Abram's side, but he motions for them to keep back again. He's got this. All but the dumbest one obey.

"Our reward, Abram?" the man asks.

Abram shoves the man away and keeps his attention on his prey. "You thought you could outsmart me?" he asks Darius.

The man Abram shoved doesn't leave well enough alone. "Mr. Job, with respect —"

"Do not address me!"

"Sir, we just want what was promised to us."

"Your reward is the good you've done." Abram smirks. "For Zalmon."

Mourning the life-changing rewards he believed he was in for, the man jumps on Abram, who, with nothing more than a look, summons the other three to turn rabidly on their dim-witted comrade. They hoist him and remove him from Abram's office, kicking and screaming.

News bursts on a screen. The all-too-familiar photo of Darius is displayed. A newscaster reads, "Breaking news this evening in Zalmon. Violent Datura Darius Anah has been detained by the good people of Zalmon. Stay tuned for more information."

RELEASE

Priya didn't even notice that she'd fallen asleep in the old Welcome Release Viewing Room. Noise on the other side of the one-way mirror wakes her up. She opens her eyes to see Zuriel preparing for an end of life.

Priya looks around the small, uninviting room. She can't help but think that with a little bit of sprucing up, the room could be opened. If Welcome Releases are so wonderful and blissful, why not? From what Priya has read, this room's never been used; it was such a waste of resources.

On the opposite side of the mirror, Zuriel leads a female client into the Welcome Release room. She's older, mid-fifties, but appears to be in very good shape.

Priya notes the look in the woman's eyes — the whites show more than usual. She looks scared and uncomfortable. Her expression is juxtaposed with Zuriel's, which is calm and almost exuberant.

Something about the clinical state of the room they're in and the cold, uninhabited space Priya is in churns her stomach. She doesn't know what compels her to take out her phone to employ a hack she heard about at school. She hits a series of commands and starts recording everything.

Zuriel taps the shoulder of the pale, trembling woman. "You're okay," she says. "This is a joyous occasion."

The woman nods in compliance more than anything. Her soft, white pajama set clings to her on account of the pools of sweat.

Zuriel points to the Welcome Release chair. "Have a seat." The chair's nothing close to the plush, new, comfy ones boasted of in Quiet End advertisements.

The woman sits.

Zuriel puts on her protective gear: hooded coveralls, a mask, boots, and gloves. The woman is completely exposed in her white cotton.

Zuriel bends down to open a code-locked bin labeled "Potassium Cyanide." She scoops some pellets from it then drops them into a basin under the woman's chair.

"Would you like me to read from the Book?" Zuriel asks.

The woman nods, her eyes watery.

Zuriel fumbles with her thick gloves but manages to open the Book to a dog-eared page.

Priya feels disgusted for the woman.

Zuriel reads, "We praise those who embrace the final moments of this life in Zalmon, knowing of the blessed eternity thereafter. We are not here simply because we fear a Natural

Death. We are here to revel blissfully in the Zalmon promise."

Zuriel closes the Book, then, rather than set it on the table, she plops it on the woman's lap. The woman jumps.

Priya zooms in as Zuriel tightens four leather straps to restrain the woman in the chair. Zuriel, noticing that the woman has soiled her white pants, frowns and nods patronizingly. "Just try to take some deep breaths," she says. "For a faster Release."

Priya nearly drops her phone but steadies it again. Her eyes flood with tears; she doesn't even know this poor woman.

Zuriel seems to be trying to satisfy a mental checklist. Fasten the straps — check. Close the pellets bin — check. Lock it — check. Assess the integrity of the rubber seal of the room's door — check.

Zuriel taps the woman on her arm one last time. The woman's bottom lip quivers, and tears run from her eyes.

Zuriel exits the room. The woman is alone.

Zuriel closes the airtight door then checks its rubber sealing on this side too — check. She continues to follow procedure.

A flick of a switch. Inside the Welcome Release room, concentrated sulfuric acid pours down a thin tube to the basin of the pellets under the chair.

The chemicals react, and hydrogen cyanide fills the small room.

The woman's breathing quickens. It's shallow, panicked.

Priya winces. She wants to capture it all, but she cannot stand to watch. She wants to save the woman, but she fears the obvious toxicity of the gas; she's not a hero.

After minutes of the torture, the woman still gasps for air. She screams for help. She begs for her children and grandchildren. She screams out for Zuriel … for anyone … to stop her Release.

Minutes pass …

The woman drools uncontrollably. She wails. She's incomprehensible. She convulses.

Priya cries, hard. She struggles to focus. She falls to the ground, curls up, and bawls on the cold, hard Welcome Release Viewing Room floor.

CONFESS

Zalmon has one prison cell, and it's always been empty. There's never been a reason to incarcerate someone. The governing system, along with the Book and effective propaganda, have made the people of Zalmon completely compliant.

Two guards throw Darius into the cell. He hits the cement wall and moans in pain. He falls limply to the ground. One of the guards slams the cell door shut. The clang reverberates down the empty hallway and echoes back into Darius's soul.

Abram walks into the prison and stands just outside Darius's cell. He watches as the boy lies motionless on the freezing floor, beaten to a pulp.

"I've never been in here before, Darius." Abram looks at the centipedes along the walls and the mounds of rat feces everywhere. "This prison's always been such a sore spot for me." He looks at the small sink, the thin cot, the barred window, and the small hole in the corner where Darius is supposed to relieve himself.

"You have everything you need," Abram says; he starts to walk away but turns back. "The difference between someone like you and someone like me, son, is faith. I learned the secrets of Zalmon through my father, and I devoted my life to protecting them." Abram holds onto the bars. "My life!" he yells.

Then he walks away.

Mahlah sleeps on the floor in Aysa's office. Someone placed a blanket over her and rolled up a sweater to put under her head.

Noah sits guard right in the same room, beside the door, and watches her sleep.

Aysa unlocks the door and walks in.

The noise wakes Mahlah up. Noah stands and gives Aysa a dirty look. "The poor kid just got to sleep," he grumbles.

Aysa doesn't want to hear it right now. He's conflicted and tired. "I've been looking around at all the people down here." He glances at Jir, who's cozy under a blanket as white as his hair in the corner. "For the first time, it hit me ... we all flourish. None of us has ever Left. We don't need them. But suddenly, I've lost pride in us." He sighs. "I don't know, Noah. I think I always tried to do the right thing."

"For as long as I've known you," Noah says.

"Me too," Mahlah says, intent on contributing to the conversation, unaware of the humor in her words. The two men chuckle.

"I'm almost forty-six years old," Aysa says, knowing full well he's nearly disposable in the eyes of Zalmon.

"You've lived a good life," Noah reminds him.

"I've misjudged all Leavers. Canceled their goodness on account of one move. Always secretly hoped they'd reflect, reform, and return. Gone. Forever."

"You didn't know." Noah looks at the ground and fidgets. He's a man of faith, really; he's always had to be to harvest what he could out of the unsatisfying life he's been given. The Underground is just a place where he feels a bit more like he belongs, which is all he's ever dreamed of.

"What's out there, Noah?"

Priya throws a rock through a back window at Darius's house. With some work (and cut-up hands), the hole becomes big enough for Priya to slip through.

She runs straight upstairs and passes Mahlah's bedroom. Flashes of that traumatizing night render her legs useless for a moment, but she pulls herself together. She guesses that the next bedroom may be Darius's. She's wrong — it's Sela's. Priya closes the door quickly to shut the memories out — but not fast enough to unsee the pajama outfit Sela laid out for herself, with the full intention of sleeping in it that night.

The last room of the hallway, past the bathroom, is Darius's. It even smells like Darius: somehow like indifference, intelligence, and infectious personality. She runs over to his untidy desk and tosses a pile of laundry aside to uncover Darius's laptop. Priya takes a massive breath, plunks herself into a chair, then gets to work.

A public service announcement interrupts her train of thought as it plays, unsolicited, on the laptop and on all technology in Zalmon.

In the ad, Darius sits in solitude in the jail cell as the camera pans along his body, careful to show the disgusting conditions of the place. "As you know, thanks to the good people of Zalmon, Darius Anah has been detained." A repeat montage of happy, healthy families graces the screen. "Peace has been restored to our land." A news ticker plays beneath the real-time clip of Darius, who lies absolutely still. It reads: *Darius Anah, Violent Datura, Detained by the Good People of Zalmon.* "Tune in tonight at 8:00 p.m., when we'll broadcast a live public apology from Darius Anah, followed by..." The reporter stops to reread their notes in surprise. They continue, "Followed by his gruesome ... Natural Death." The reporter looks off camera. The live feed swipes to a pre-recorded clip of Abram.

"I am an average, everyday man — Darius's mother's Second Match. His mother, incidentally, has decided to Leave. She could not handle her diseased son after he broke into our invaluable Central Processing department and intercepted the Zalmon gift of his Death Date. Darius chose a Natural Death, and a Natural Death he shall receive."

The shocked reporter takes a moment to compose themselves. "That's right, folks. We will witness history tonight as we gather to watch the dreadfully feared organic demise of Darius Anah. Tune in at 8:00 p.m."

DENY

It's business as usual at the Zalmon Communications Center. The workers notify the people of Zalmon of the breaking story updates. The whole town is wired for the controlled, immediate, intrusive feed, whether they like it or not.

Priya has snuck in, joining in line with a group of high school students on a tour of the Center. In her clenched right hand is a small USB stick.

As the group tours through the broadcasting rooms, the students ask questions of the directors, assistants, and producers. They poke and prod some unplugged mixing boards, teleprompters, and microphones. As they peruse a wall of famous broadcasters they've seen over the years, Priya slips out and runs down the hall into a vacant stall in the women's restroom. She locks the metal door with the small hook-and-loop clasp, stands on top of the toilet, and crouches down. Audio and visuals blast onto her cellphone.

It's the same feed to every house.

Every electronic billboard.

Every restaurant and grocery store, where all the patrons are glued to it.

Every monitor in Quiet End, where Zuriel stands watching.

And throughout the Underground, where everyone is on pins and needles for the fate of their new friend.

It is eight o'clock — time for Darius's public apology and, unbeknownst to all of them, his murder.

Mahlah paces next to Aysa and Noah. Her head is in her hands, and tears stream down her cheeks. "We should be there. We should be right there in Town Square to jump in and save him!"

Noah holds her tight in his warm embrace and shields her eyes from the incessant trail of words at the bottom of the screen.

Tune In at 8:00 p.m. Public Apology and Natural Death of Datura Darius Anah …

But the live broadcast is running late.

Darius sits on his creaky cot, huddled in the corner, oblivious to the recent news. Abram enters the prison, impatient for Darius's vital public apology and the big ending.

"There's our little superstar," Abram announces.

Darius shoots Abram the finger.

Abram ignores it. He looks down the hall and eyes a small glass of liquid in front of one of his henchmen. The man takes a powdery substance and pours it into the glass before stirring it. As he removes the metal spoon from the mixture, the silver disintegrates all over the floor.

Abram winks.

A television producer nods to signal that everything is in place in Town Square for the broadcast.

Abram checks with Darius. "Have you rehearsed?"

Darius nods.

Abram needs to be sure. "Let me hear it first."

Monotone, Darius delivers the line, "Abram Job, your fearless leader, is a crock of shit."

Abram slams his palms against the prison bars. "Warn him!" he orders. Two men enter Darius's cell and pound him with tight fists to his abdomen. "Avoid his face! Yeah! That's it! Just like that! More!"

Darius doesn't even scream anymore. He just makes himself go limp and takes the blows. He has no more tears to cry. No more yells to yawp and no more gusto to give.

"Enough!" Abram shouts.

The men leave the cell and re-lock it.

Abram and Darius stare each other down. "Let me remind you, Darius," Abram says in a low voice, "your friend Priya Tiras has been spared on account of your promise to cooperate."

Darius looks at the ground.

"As for your sister, one slipup will leave me with no choice."

Darius doesn't look up.

"Now!" Abram commands.

"I am Darius Anah —"

"Stand up, boy!"

Darius slowly stands up. "I am Darius Anah. I have caused the people of Zalmon grief. I spent my life miserable from the pain my father caused me when he Left. I was only twelve years old. He did not die, like I told many of you. I only said that because I was seeking revenge for my pain, and it was easier to believe that than it was to think he just Left." Darius stops.

"More!"

Darius slowly walks forward until only the prison bars separate him from Abram. He finishes his spiel. "I have no access to any truths beyond those in the Book. Zalmon is what it always was — a place of peace, contentment, and comfort with all the bliss of a Welcome Release at Quiet End."

Abram hesitates then slowly unlocks the cell. His henchmen pop in to restrain Darius, then they take him out to get settled on a stage in the middle of Town Square.

Priya finally exits the washroom at the Communications Center. She has the USB stick in one hand and a short kitchen knife she stole from Darius's house in the other. She makes her way down the hallway to the newsroom.

On the stage in Town Square, Darius sits strapped to a chair. Abram sits back in the shadows. He leaves nothing to chance, especially seeing the massive crowd of onlookers who have showed up to witness the event. The camera operator zooms in on Darius to prepare for transmission to the thousands who didn't make it.

Back at the Communications Center, the workers responsible for the feed don't see Priya behind them in the dark room.

Shaking, Priya raises the sharp knife and holds its tip against the director's neck.

"Out!" Priya yells at the others. "Except you." She nods to the assistant director.

A couple of brave workers move to save the director, so Priya draws a drop of his blood with a push of the knife.

"Do what she says," the director yelps.

They do.

"Go lock the door behind them, then sit back down," Priya orders the assistant director. After he's done so, Priya hands him the USB. "Put it in," Priya says.

The assistant looks at his boss.

Priya doesn't like that. She musters the strength to draw more blood.

"Do it!" the director says.

In the company of her colleagues at Quiet End, Zuriel is tuned in, arms crossed, fuming for Darius's apology but resolute about his death. She's never been so embarrassed in her life.

In the Underground, Mahlah's watery eyes widen as she steals a glance at her brother on the screen, bound mid-stage.

The on-location director preps Darius and a small camera crew with, "Quiet on the set. Ready in five ... four ... three ... two ..." A red light prompts Darius to start. He stares directly into the lens, takes a deep breath, and speaks.

"I am Darius Anah. I have caused the people of Zalmon grief —"

Priya cues the director, and he nods to his assistant to press the button that will alter the feed from Town Square to the video on Priya's USB. Darius's live apology is replaced by the transmission of —

Priya's commercial.

A familiar montage of happy, healthy families graces the screen. "Zalmon. Where we thought life was good." A new picture of Darius comes onscreen. He appears interested in something off-screen. "Darius Anah infiltrated the system illegally, yes. Why? To stop a Death Card. Not his; his little sister's." An image of Mahlah fades in. She's terribly sweet and innocent looking. Her hair is up in pigtails — Sela's favorite style for her. "On December fifteenth, her supposed Death Date, which she would have averted with a Welcome Release at Quiet End, Mahlah Anah did not suffer a Natural Death." The Zalmon Medical Center comes onscreen. "Doctors can't predict when we will die with certainty! And *sick*? 'Sick' is defined as weak physically, because something is wrong within. 'Sick' costs Zalmon. 'Old' costs Zalmon." A picture of Quiet End appears, followed by a montage of happy clients reading, exercising, and painting. "Like all of you, I believed in Zalmon and thought it had my best interests at heart. I felt the peace and comfort of Quiet End. I worked there, for crying out loud." Priya's footage of the woman from the gas chamber plays uncensored and uncut with the words *Actual Welcome Release* on a repeat ticker underneath. "That was all before Darius Anah infiltrated my system."

Zuriel watches in shock.

Mahlah winces at the screen, covers her eyes again, and cries, "I can't look!"

Aysa and Noah are engrossed by the brutal execution continuing onscreen.

In the Communications Center, the director slowly stands up — Priya lets him. He fights the urge to turn his head from the suffering on the screen. The assistant director lowers his head; he can't stomach it.

All those who aren't at Town Square — the people in the restaurants, grocery stores, homes, or anywhere else with a screen or their phone — are seeing the same thing.

On the stage, Darius is just finishing his apology, perfectly executed, to the delight of Abram, the crew, and the entranced audience, who are hanging on Darius's last words.

"… a place of peace, contentment, and comfort with all the bliss of a Welcome Release at Quiet End."

The camera operators stop recording. They signal a thumbs-up to Abram. "That's a wrap," the on-location director hollers.

Abram motions for them to keep rolling as he nudges his henchmen to fetch the glass of liquid.

But it's not where it was. It's already in the hands of one of the crew and on its way to Darius as he trembles, parched.

Darius looks at the ground and cries. Two men unstrap him so that he can manage to drink the potion they concocted. They laugh to themselves.

Darius, oblivious, takes the drink that's handed to him by a woman. He can't help but notice what look like tattoos peeking out from the wrist of her white blouse.

"You must be thirsty," she says.

Darius remembers those eyes. He lifts the cup to his lips.

Abram can't hold back his smile.

The crowd wonders when the big ending will be.

Darius downs the full glass to the very last drop.

Abram waits. His phone rings. He sends it to voicemail.

The henchmen wait. They expect Darius to die from the inside out.

Abram's phone rings again. To voicemail.

"What is going on?" he asks.

A whole lot of nothing. The crowd waits, growing impatient; a few of them start for home. Abram notices.

His phone rings again.

He reaches into his pocket to answer it. The voice on the other end blasts him. Abram's eyes widen. He hangs up and turns on the news.

He catches the tail end of Priya's commercial: A bug-eyed, soiled, and excrement-laden woman in a white outfit convulses uncontrollably and drools on the screen. She heaves her final, violent breaths while a ticker repeats under the footage.

Darius Anah knows.

A group of men shoot down the corridors of the Communications Center and burst through the newsroom door. They point guns at Priya. She drops the knife and raises her hands to surrender.

"You think she's the problem here?" The director wipes the blood from his neck and calls them off.

At Quiet End, Zuriel stumbles blindly down the hallway, where everything is in chaos. Some clients start to pack their things. Some clients stay in their beds.

Zuriel finds a wall, leans against it, and slowly falls to the ground as she cradles the Book in her hands.

LEAVE

In the wee hours of the night, Mahlah, Aysa, and Noah climb up from the Underground and walk.

They don't know how it happened, but it seems like suddenly there's a relatively huge group of followers behind them — a couple of thousand people — some from the Underground and some from above.

They're on their way to see Darius.

Everyone feels uneasy and confused. No one knows who to look at or what to say. Matias stands behind Mahlah, feeling some strange need to protect her until she's back with kin. Jir, the oldest person in Zalmon, sets the pace.

They all walk along the road's edge, where a few hardcover books are strewn and strange little creatures that don't live further inland crawl and hop. The overhead lights of the City Border are not far from the prison, which they're closing in on.

Darius sits in his lonely cell, completely unaware of the night's events beyond those he was part of; heedless of the swell of people less than a mile away — a swell that keeps growing. Here, it's eerily quiet: no guards, no Abram. Darius thinks he hears a faint sound in the distance but he shrugs it off.

Meanwhile, at Quiet End, a car pulls up front and barely misses some people who are fleeing the building. Abram rushes out of the car and speeds, as if in a trance, into his establishment.

Darius tries to lie down. He cannot. He tosses and turns, ruminating over the damage he did to those he cares about. He worries about where Mahlah is and if someone will take care of her now that he's gone. He imagines the worst ways in which Abram could plan to dispose of him.

Darius is sure he hears something this time. He stands at his cell bars, thinking the noise stems from down the hall, but he sees that all technology is off and there's no one in sight.

He walks back to sit on his hard cot, but then he realizes that the sounds are coming from outside. He runs over to his tiny, barred window and jumps up to look out, but he's not tall enough.

He surrenders to his cot.

The murmur gets louder and louder.

At Quiet End, the scurrying continues for hours.

Past the panic, past the offices, and past the painting room and library, Abram arrives and slams into the Welcome Release room. He spots Zuriel there, on the floor, holding the Book.

Abram grabs it from her hands and pulls her to follow him; she allows it.

In the cell, it's unmistakable now. The ruckus is a crowd. A chanting crowd. The words are shouted in unison, but Darius still can't make them out. He's scared. He believes it's a mob on its way to hang him. He cowers on the bare cot.

At Quiet End, Abram lowers himself into the Welcome Release chair.

With a look, Zuriel asks him if he's sure.

"There's no point now." His phone rings perpetually. Zuriel peeks at its caller ID, and it reads *Father*.

Zuriel goes to strap Abram's arms in, but he won't have it.

Zuriel bends down to open the locked bin and scoops some potassium cyanide pellets into the small basin under the chair. She opens the Book but then closes it. She knows this part by heart: "We praise those who embrace the final moments of this life in Zalmon, knowing of the blessed eternity thereafter. We are not here simply because we fear a Natural Death. We are here to revel blissfully —"

Abram grabs the Book from her hands. He places it on his lap. "Let's just get this over with, shall we?" Without hesitation, Zuriel does as she's told. She glides her fingers over the door seal before she leaves the room to trigger the Release.

Alone in the room, Abram's life flashes before his eyes until the gas hisses, and he takes long, calm, deep breaths.

⌒

The noise outside Darius's cell boils over. He's done submitting to fear; he needs to face what's out there. He welcomes his impending doom, feeling it's deserved. He wishes to decipher the chanting.

Darius pulls at his cot even though it's fastened to the wall. He yanks at it, shoves it, pushes it, and screams for more strength. The cot finally breaks free. Darius flings it over to the window. Standing on the cot, he's just tall enough to see —

The most amazing sight. Thousands of people march toward the prison, unified, chanting: "Darius Anah knows … Darius Anah knows …"

They are led by none other than Mahlah, Aysa, and Noah. Darius can't breathe. He gasps for air, confused. For a split second, he looks for Priya before remembering she never wants to see him again.

Darius hears commotion inside the prison now. He continues to look out the window, fearing this is his last chance to see something beautiful.

Behind him, his cell bars creak open. He braces himself for the worst. The bars close again. He can hear guards' feet walk away, yet he senses he's not alone.

"Darius."

He freezes. He slowly turns his head.

His eyes meet Priya's.

"What are you doing here?" Darius yells at her. "Go!"

"I've done something bad."

"What?" Darius asks. "What did you do?"

"I …"

"Spit it out Priya! What did you do?"

"I … I saved you," she says as she leans against the cell bars to show Darius that they're not locked.

Darius stares at the bars. Then he stares at Priya. He's confused but enthralled. He walks up to her. Never in his life has he wanted to kiss her more.

Priya turns her head. "There are so many people out there. Not my mom — I can't get ahold of her for the life of me — but so many people, Darius. They're all waiting for you. You can't let them down." She takes his hand and leads him out of his cell.

Darius stands dumbfounded in front of the sea of people. They're silent, waiting breathlessly for him to speak.

Nothing is coming to mind.

Mahlah walks up to him and gives him a massive hug. It triggers memories of Grandpa Felix at Quiet End. The rage Darius felt that day fuels him now.

"I'm Darius Anah," he starts. The crowd erupts. He waves them off to stop the praise. "I'm Darius Anah, and I have caused the people of Zalmon grief."

A hush falls over the crowd.

"I know that the things I discovered are sad — my heart's been ripped out. I know you're hurting too. I can see it in your eyes. It's the same look I could see in people's eyes for too long."

Mahlah knows he means their mother's eyes.

"I did a selfish thing when I stopped my sister's Death Date." The crowd erupts again. Darius is shocked by their insistent cheers and applause. Once it calms: "I spent so many years hating my father for Leaving. How could he? Didn't he love me?

Didn't he love my sister? My mother? What a selfish bastard to do such a thing. But now … now, I want to Leave."

The crowd goes silent — they didn't expect that. Darius questions if it was the right thing to say, but he went with his heart.

Aysa's never been prouder of someone.

Darius yells, "Forget the Underground. You're treating yourselves like vermin."

As the crowd processes that and slowly concurs, a trickle of claps grows into thunderous applause. Priya runs up to him. "Me too, Darius. I want to go with you, and I want to find my father!"

It's bittersweet — they are words he'd normally faint over, but it is painfully obvious that no one told Priya about Leavers yet. Maybe no one told the lot of them. The weight of the world is back on Darius's shoulders.

Priya screeches when she spots her mother coming at her from deep within the crowd. "Mom!" she yells. "Let's Leave. Let's just … offer forgiveness and go find Dad."

"Folks," Darius starts, "I need you all to know something that may bring immense heartache." He looks right at Priya. "No one has ever Left Zalmon."

Mahlah, Noah, and Aysa drop their heads.

Priya doesn't know what he means, but she senses a grave declaration.

"Leaving's been fabricated by Zalmon to demonize Natural Death so you'd live the way they wanted you to live and die when and how they wanted you to die, all for the glory of their bottom line."

Private conversations break out. Darius waits for them to subside.

"Part of living is dying one day, and on rare occasions, people go unexpectedly, despite Zalmon's elaborate schemes to avoid it."

Priya cries. Her mother consoles her.

"Anyone who witnessed those deaths was doomed to a micro-surveilled life — Daturas." Darius winces at the word. Many people in the crowd break down in tears. Some because it's an awakening. Some because they've been Datura for years and are finally freed from their confines.

Darius can't handle the sadness in Priya and Mahlah's eyes.

"When people die, we may assume they're gone forever, but …" Darius looks over at Noah. "They're not."

Noah beams.

"Their bodies merely change form." Darius points up to the stars in the night sky. "They're all around us in new ways." He looks over at the real trees, so close he feels like he can touch them. "They'll always be with us wherever we go."

Darius steps down and walks up to Priya. "Maybe he's right here." He bops her on the nose. She manages a tiny smile through tears.

From within the crowd, Darius shouts, "Darius Anah does not know! I know very, very little. But whatever is out there has to be better than what I'm ready to leave behind. I want to be free to live how I want to live and with whom I want to live." Mahlah and Priya are at his sides.

The crowd cheers. Darius starts walking. "Don't follow me," he says. "Let's lead each other and be there for each other and see what our future holds. The good, the bad, the easy, the hard, the right, the wrong — all of it."

With Darius in the middle, the crowd surges right past the sole border guard, who has finally stopped smiling.

As they step over the final edge of Zalmon and into the unknown —

Mahlah peeks over at Matias, who winks at her.

Noah looks forward to discovering who he is and the depths of what he can offer.

Aysa sees a rainbow in the creeping, dewy sunrise.

A mourning dove flutters its wings then perches atop the first real tree Darius touches.

Priya can't take it anymore. She grabs his shoulder and whips him around. They stare into each other's eyes.

Time stands still.

"Thank you, Priya." Darius means it with his whole heart.

"You shouldn't look at me like that."

Slowly, very slowly, a smile spreads across Darius's lips.

They meet halfway and kiss the most perfect kiss.

ACKNOWLEDGEMENTS

Sometime around 2010, I woke up from a deep sleep. Death Date Cards on your birthday — I said the words aloud, then fell back to sleep. Most ideas I get in the middle of the night come and go. I always think I'll remember them but I don't, and on the very rare occasions that I write them down, they're gibberish come morning. However, this idea didn't fade. It gained momentum through the years and held real estate in my imagination for a very long time.

And then one day, I wrote the story.

Defy is very different from my debut novel, *White Lies*. The worlds are different. The plots are different. The messages are different. But they both come from a place within me that champions characters in difficult situations who find the inner strength and social circle to pull through, despite the odds and obstacles.

My life has been much the same.

I believe that the heart of this novel is the relationship between a boy and his mom, a boy and his little sister, and a boy and his true love. I have a son who changed the trajectory of my life and made me better the day he was born. He proved that I could break a cycle if I mustered the courage and did the work. When I had his little sister, she floored all of us, proving that our capacity for love knows no limits. I continue to watch Isaac and Ava discover themselves and navigate life. I'm in constant awe. I thank them for their unconditional love – and my love for them is unparalleled.

I'll never forget the moment *Defy's* impact hit me. A great teaching colleague of mine, Paul Lorenz, had read the screenplay version to his intermediate students at Steele Street Public School. One day, I was walking along a row of lockers and came across a blue binder — Gareth's binder, I think — and the title *Defy* was doodled on it in powerful, block graffiti letters. The story resonated and that was all I ever wanted. I'm thankful to Paul and those kids who, more than a decade later, are *Defy's* lifelong promoters.

What's the point of something special like this happening, if you don't have people to share it with? I am blessed with a loyal, entertaining, loving and constructive social circle. My best friends are family to me. In addition to them, my siblings and extended family watch over me in the absence of our deceased parents as I navigate this roller-coaster dream catching. Also, many of my colleagues have taken special interest in my endeavors and are friends beyond the classroom. People cannot accomplish grand things in isolation, this I'm sure of.

DCB (the imprint of Cormorant Books) launched *White Lies* then subsequently laid the foundation for *Defy*. I am humbled by their commitment to my stories and their boutique but mighty business. Thank you to Barry, Marc, the Sarahs, Luckshika, Fei, and all the others who work passionately and tirelessly to bring great literature to enthusiasts.

A lot of editing love went into *Defy*'s novel journey, mostly at the fingertips of the talented, intuitive, and motivational Barry Jowett, furthered by the tenacious copyediting of Andrea Waters. Special thanks to my Ava for her early and keen eye on the manuscript (and for being my incomparable cheerleader). Also thanks to super JB grade 8 editors Nicolas and Nina who took peeks at it to learn more about a career I believe they'd excel at.

Thank you for the professional and inspirational guidance from two authors who took time out of their intense schedules to offer me words of wisdom and encouragement at pivotal points in my process: Eric Walters and Romi Mondi. As well on my screenwriting side, in what I hope will become a motion picture, I appreciate the furtherance of my writing through manager Andrea Dimity and our friend, David Boxerbaum. Financially, the Recommender Grants for *Defy* from Cormorant, ECW, and the Ontario Arts Council were a godsend.

Thank you so much to you — the reader — for diving into *Defy* and any of my other works. Without you, my stories would be … nothing.

Finally, I acknowledge that Port Colborne, the land on which I live, work & draw inspiration from, is the traditional territory of the Haudenosaunee and Anishinaabe peoples. It is covered by the Upper Canada treaties and is within the land protected by the Dish with One Spoon Wampum agreement. I am of Métis descent on both my mother and father's side (Algonquin

Huronne Wendat on my mother's side and from the research I've done, the same on my father's side and also from the Essex area). Growing up, no one in my family talked about our background and now, unfortunately all my parents and grandparents are deceased so the learning is in my hands. Ever since I became aware of Residential Schools and educated myself on the terrible treatment of Indigenous peoples, I have been committed to making a difference where and when I can. I mourn our missed opportunities to follow the lead of how the Indigenous care for our environment and prioritize society. I am proud to say that a lot of the ways in which I live, parent, teach, and express myself artistically stem from this deep-rooted culture.

Sara de Waard is an author, screenwriter, and educator of Métis descent and is currently in the process of exploring her family's heritage. Her debut novel, *White Lies*, won the 2022 ETFO Writer's Award for Women. After completing her BA in Radio and Television from Toronto Metropolitan University and a stint in London, ON, de Waard returned to her hometown of Port Colborne, ON, where she currently lives with her kids.

We acknowledge the sacred land on which Cormorant Books operates. It has been a site of human activity for 15,000 years. This land is the territory of the Huron-Wendat and Petun First Nations, the Seneca, and most recently, the Mississaugas of the Credit River. The territory was the subject of the Dish With One Spoon Wampum Belt Covenant, an agreement between the Iroquois Confederacy and Confederacy of the Ojibway and allied nations to peaceably share and steward the resources around the Great Lakes. Today, the meeting place of Toronto is still home to many Indigenous people from across Turtle Island. We are grateful to have the opportunity to work in the community, on this territory.

We are also mindful of broken covenants and the need to strive to make right with all our relations.